A Christmas Reborn

A New Era in Scrooge's Redemption

Scott A. Johnson

A Christmas Reborn

A NEW ERA IN SCROOGE'S REDEMPTION

Scott A. Johnson

A Christmas Reborn: A New Era in Scrooge's Redemption

Cover design: Scott A. Johnson
Cover Copyright © 2025, by Scott A. Johnson

Some cover and interior images were created using Google's Gemini generative AI during May 2025.

ISBN-13: 979-8988720676

Published by Scott A. Johnson Professional Writing Services, LLC: Orem, UT
Discover more books by Scott A. Johnson at authorscott.com/shop/

Table of Contents

Table of Contents

Chapter 1: A Changed Man

The Scrooge of times past lay dead as a doornail. His old, cranky, miserly, uncaring former self existed no more, laid to rest with all the coldness and cruelty once defining him.

In his stead had risen a new man, an effusive man, wholly transformed and charitable, greatly benevolent and merciful. He had come to be regarded as one of the most generous gentlemen in all of London Town. Whoever would have thought it? But it was true, as strange as that may sound.

Nowadays, he was considered a beacon of goodwill in a city often gripped by greed and despair.

Gone was the shadow of the miser who once had walked these streets, his visage bearing a scowl deep enough to curdle the jolliest caroler's cheer, making small children turn and flee.

In his place walked a soul renewed, whose step seemed lighter, as though the weight of his former avarice had been lifted by miraculous, unseen hands. And so it was that on a crisp December morning—the kind on which the sun's pale light spilled over the cobblestones and danced frenetically on frost-rimed windows, promising a day cold enough to pinch the noses of schoolchildren and stiffen market traders' fingertips—that this reformed Scrooge was making his way through the city.

The usual commotion of rattling carriages and vendors' cries filled the air, but there was something else too, a peculiar warmth seemingly following in his wake. Cane in hand, armed with a smile broad enough to disarm even the most cynical passerby, Ebenezer Scrooge strode amongst his fellow Londoners, a figure beloved and inspiring, not any longer feared and reviled.

Absent was that crotchety miser of yesteryear, his name whispered with contempt behind closed doors, cursed by the poor who had suffered his heartless rebukes when he had named them lazy, good-for-nothing scoundrels who would never earn a penny in their lives by hard work.

In the near decade since his fateful encounter with the spirits of Christmas Past, Ebenezer Scrooge had metamorphosed into the personification of generosity and humbleness. His tall frame, once stooping under the weight of greed and regret, was bearing a nimble, sprightly air.

His cheeks, once dull, sallow and sunken, were glowing with health, and his eyes, formerly as cold as unlit coals, shone with genuine goodwill. These days, he was filled with so much cheer that he did not know how to contain it, going about the city crying out, "Such a wonderful life!"

Indeed, so cheerful had he become that many disbelieved it, cynically whispering when they spotted him ambling their way, "Here he comes again, the 'hark, all giving is good' fool." They said this in playful teasing and utter bewilderment, of course. For Londoners had fostered a genuine affection for this man now redeemed.

Clad in a fine coat draping elegantly over his shoulders, Scrooge moved with a veritable spring in his step and a lightness belying his age, exuding a spirit so effervescent that one might have mistaken him for a man still drinking from youth's fountain. His crinkly skin refused to give in to age now; he was determined to be the most vibrant, cheeriest, non-crotchety elder in all of London.

"Good morning to you, ma'am," he cried as he went, raising his cane to the air in a show of joviality. "Good morning, sir! 'Tis fine weather we greet on this day, is it not? Ah, a most glorious day indeed."

Warmth and familiarity had become fine bedfellows on his demeanor, solitude's chilly grasp having flitted away as if for good. Somehow, old, grumpy Scrooge had shed his infamously bad temper, leaving behind the ghost of a man who previously had shunned life itself.

***

Today, as on most mornings, Scrooge had a destination. He was on his way to visit the Cratchit family, who had lately become as dear to him as his own kith and kin. Bob Cratchit, no longer merely his clerk but now also his trusted business partner, awaited him at the modest but cheerful home Scrooge had helped him secure. Indeed, Scrooge's own fortunes had accrued of late, not through hoarding but through wise investments guided by a newfound sense of stewardship. Yet he took no credit for his prosperity, instead marveling at the many blessings God had given to him.

As he approached the Cratchit home just days away from Christmas Eve, the laughter of children spilled out into the streets like the melodious chime of church bells calling the faithful to Evensong.

With a now familiar warmth in his heart, he paused for a moment to listen, delight growing within him like the first rays of dawn piercing winter's fog. Tiny Tim, that once-fragile, sickly boy whose delicate health had posed endless worry and heartache, now stood before the world as a lively lad of seventeen, his spirit buoyant and irrepressible. The shades of despair once cast over the lad by London's soot-laden skies, heavy with their grim pallor of coal smoke and the relentless march of callous industry, had dissipated, leaving but the faintest memory of grim times gone by.

The previously obvious bowing of Tiny Tim's lower limbs, a cruel testament to rickets, had also been miraculously reversed; Scrooge, in a great gesture of heartfelt generosity, had summoned the age's finest medics, employing them to guide young Tim through a transformative health regimen.

The healing properties of cod liver oil, long since expounded in all the newspapers and daubed large on the sides of red-brick factory walls, had dispatched the perils of vitamin D deficiency that had been plaguing the lad so cruelly. Now, Tim was standing tall and straight like any other fine young man of his age, radiating a vigor most extraordinary for one so young.

The boy's smile possessed a warmth capable of brightening the dimmest dungeon; his sweet but newly broken voice rang out above the household's joyous laughter as he led his siblings in a spirited rendition of a carol. Even this, the good Scrooge himself had taught to them.

In that moment, encircled by the warmth of family and festivity, the spirit of Christmas enveloped them all. In Scrooge's heart, a light shone brightly, transcending the vile misery of his former days.

One of the Cratchit younglings, quick as a startled mouse, had spied Scrooge lurking just outside.

Wearing a grin as wide as his eager face, the boy had flung open the humble portal to welcome their anticipated guest to their abode at the top of a steep cobbled hill; it sat in the city's midst, an iron handrail traversing its middle, splitting the hill into an 'up' and a 'down' side. A walker had to cling to that rail for dear life. Huffing and puffing, Scrooge made his way up steadily, and through one of the tiny round windows in the home's front room, the Cratchit boy must have spotted him coming.

Scrooge took his time getting to the top, leaving the Cratchits enough minutes to brew a pot of tea on the big iron stove, also to tidy away the things over which the elderly man always stumbled.

God knew, Scrooge would need plenty of sustenance once he arrived. Getting up that infernal hill was always hard. But going down, its notorious steepness could sweep a man off his feet and send him careening down the cobbles, returning him to the bottom in an array of bloody bruises and curses.

Today, Scrooge clung to that iron rail, intent on tackling the appalling hill climb like an intrepid mountaineer. Nothing at all could keep him from his good friends and neighbors these days.

"Mr. Scrooge! It's about time you visited us!" the boy called out before immediately returning to belting out the angelic hymn indoors. The child looked like a cherub, all pink, chubby, and rosy.

"Bless my soul!" Scrooge exclaimed, his breath forming clouds in the cold air. "A choir fit for angels, and all under one roof. I swear, it is a miracle on our good Lord's green Earth!"

Bob Cratchit's countenance beamed with cheer to warm the coldest heart. He materialized in the doorway, a meaty hand extending toward Scrooge's. He offered a vigorous handshake.

"Well, well, well. Mr. Scrooge! What an unexpected pleasure, I say! Yes, what a pleasure. You're just in time to warm yourself at our hearth and to take tea. I shall just go and find my good lady to ask her to prepare and pour us some beverages. Mrs. Cratchit will be so thrilled to see you."

He dashed away, shouting, "Mrs. Cratchit! Mrs. C! A stranger comes to call! Well, not a stranger, one you will be most happy to welcome to our home. Tell me, do we have a cake to offer?"

Unfortunately, Scrooge was still in the doorway, hopping foot to foot, shivering. One never ventured over a threshold without a distinct invitation, and sadly, it had not been issued yet.

Bob Cratchit returned there shortly, wafting his hands. "Mrs. Cratchit says she can barely wait. She is going to be so, so pleased to see you once she has finished washing the scullery floor."

"And I her, my dear Bob," Scrooge replied. "I say, might I come in?"

It was a little impertinent to ask, but had he not, his boots would have frozen to the step.

"Oh, my goodness me, I beg your pardon, come in, come in! Go warm yourself by the fire."

Scrooge had thought Cratchit might completely omit to invite him in, this usually being the lady of the house's pleasure since a man would rarely answer a knock. "Such a pleasure to be here."

The warmth of the Cratchit home finally enveloped him, a stark contrast to those cruel, icy streets.

He removed his hat and gloves, and before Mr. Cratchit could dash off again to find his wife, Scrooge presented to him a parcel wrapped in plain brown paper. He winked, his kind old eyes crinkling.

"A little something for your blessed family, dear Bob. And where is our wonderful Mrs. Cratchit? Surely she hasn't banished me from her kitchen already, has she? Has she run away?"

"Never, sir!" came a voice from the back of the house. Emily Cratchit, red-cheeked and apron-clad, flour on her clothes and hands, appeared carrying a steaming pot of tea. "But I will say this: if you've brought us yet another plum pudding, I shall have to build a second larder to store it."

"Guilty as charged!" Scrooge said, laughing, setting the fat parcel on the table. "Oh dear. But one can never have too much fine pudding, particularly at Christmastime. Is that not so?" He looked at her endearingly, a mischievous spark in his eye.

"Quite so, quite so!" they enthused, their ruddy faces nodding. "Plums and prunes ... God's fare."

"Plus," said Scrooge with a wink, "I put several shillings into it. Not just one. Take care when eating as I would hate to send you or one of the children to the infirmary."

The children soon heard the chatter and entered, crowding around, their faces alight with affection. Scrooge marveled at their vitality, at the simple joy radiating from them.

He saw in their eyes a reflection of the man he had latterly become, one who chose to give not out of obligation or in the grasping hope of getting something even better in return, but out of a profound understanding of the interconnectedness of all lives. It was such a wonder to live and breathe.

Yet beneath this cheerful façade, there lingered in Scrooge's heart an ache he could not name.

It was not the old regret, the one which had purportedly been exorcised with the help of the spirits, but here it was being birthed in him, a new and unfamiliar longing.

The odd sensation surfaced only in quiet moments, when the laughter of children faded and the world grew unduly still once more. At such times, Scrooge would gaze into the flames of his hearth and wonder if his transformation had truly been enough. Was there not even more he could do?

More that he *should* do? Oddly, his efforts thus far felt so inadequate.

These questions had been plaguing him even as his days brimmed with activity.

He had become a patron of schools and hospitals, an advocate for the poor, a confidant and benefactor of the downtrodden. Yet London too was changing, its air growing heavier with the smoke of industry, the divide between rich and poor widening with each passing year.

The wealthy elite, once merely indifferent, now presented themselves as actively hostile to any notion of shared prosperity. No, sharing was never to be on the cards.

Scrooge's voice, once powerful in the halls of commerce, was increasingly becoming drowned out by the clamor of ambition and greed.

As the evening unfurled in convivial laughter, Scrooge found himself enchanted by the Cratchit family's boisterous camaraderie and always reliable tender affections.

He reveled in the merriment filling their modest home, the air also pungent with the delightful aromas of their humble feast. Each chuckle and shared story only weaved him deeper into the fabric of their joyous existence. Time itself, though painfully fleeting, seemed to be dancing a jig in sympathy with their delight. As it neared the hour for him to depart, regret began tugging at his heartstrings.

Still, all good things must come to an end, he told himself. *And when I depart here, leaving my friends behind, God will find me yet more good works to do with my hands and my benevolence.*

Stepping into the cool night air, the streets of London stretched before him like a fresh canvas.

He felt as light as a feather, buoyancy lifting his spirits, each footfall resonating with joy.

***

On one quiet evening, as Scrooge sat before his flickering fire, his thoughts wandered back to the memory of his amiable nephew, Fred.

Ah, how captivating is that lively young man, a perennial fountain of joy and inspiration!

Fred embodied the spirit of this time of year, manifesting its unyielding cheer as naturally as the holly adorned the bustling streets. This was Yuletide. Fred's laughter, though, was infectious all year round, as if intent on melting away the frost and icicles. With his ever-bright disposition, Fred had never uttered an unkind word in his young life, each syllable from his lips a testament to optimism and feeling for his fellow man. Fred radiated joy, even as the world spiraled into darkness.

It had been young Fred who'd unwittingly become a catalyst guiding Scrooge toward good change, reminding him of the possibilities of redemption and the power of love. Alas, his persistence has paid off, and Scrooge now stood as a testament to Fred's doggedness.

Fred's steadfast commitment to delight, even amid life's vicissitudes, had sparked longing in Scrooge's heart. It was a desire for connection, for belonging, for the glory of kindness and kinship.

Never would the Scrooge of old have entertained the thought that one day, he might hurl open his front door to welcome the whole world inside … or as many as would fit in the cramped hallway.

Never would he have imagined giving a hearty welcome to anyone.

Yet, there it was; his boy, his nephew, had upturned Scrooge's world, setting it on its head.

Fred's beloved wife Lily, with her gentle nature, and their delightful children filled with youthful and cheeky exuberance, had for some time been frequent visitors to Scrooge's home. There, they imbued its austere corners with life and laughter, unearthing joyous memories buried beneath the weight of Scrooge's misgivings.

Even this elderly miser could not resist their infectious exuberance and positivity.

Despite their persistent cheerfulness, however, the specter of apprehension gnawed at him.

Something was beginning to cause consternation beyond all description.

With each passing year under the wholesome influence of these good people, Scrooge had become increasingly aware that time, the relentless and unyielding master of all, was the single entity from which no mortal could escape. Time came along to take them all in the end. Rich or poor, cheerful or downbeat, convivial or selfishly introspective … Father Time came. The Grim Reaper showed up.

As these thoughts spiraled into dark corners, an ever-present fear gripped him.

Anxiousness had been born, anxiety for the futures of Fred and Lily, also for the family of the Cratchits, whom he had gradually begun to acknowledge as dear to his heart.

His anxieties were also for the city he loved, which was teetering on the precipice of despair.

In a certain dark moment, seated by the fire and witnessing the encroaching shadows of regret, Scrooge felt strong stirrings of a desire for transformation.

They had been sown long ago by his dear nephew's interminable joyfulness.

In the midst of these musings one night, a hefty knock came at the door.

Startled, Scrooge rose, swiftly opening up. He threw the door wide.

A young messenger was standing there on the doorstep, shivering and holding a letter.

"For you, sir," the out-of-breath boy said, his teeth chattering.

Scrooge took the letter, pressing a small silver coin into the boy's hand.

"Go warm yourself, lad. And thank you."

Giving thanks to any mortal soul had never been in his nature. But now, his chest glowed with all the unbridled effusiveness of a heart that found itself willing to give.

The letter bore the seal of Fred's household. With trembling fingers, Scrooge sliced open the fine parchment envelope with his silvered letter opener, reading the words intent on shattering his peace.

Dearest Fred has been taken gravely ill, stricken with scarlatina, that dire and dreadful fever.

I beseech you, please come at once. He asks after his uncle like no other.

Yours ever,

Lily.

***

By the next morning, having traveled swiftly through the night by coach and four, he was sitting at Fred's bedside, where Lily sat clutching her husband's hand, looking tearful and all too pale.

Fred's once-vibrant countenance was just as pallid, his breaths labored, and an all-too-familiar scarlet rash bloomed floridly across his face and neck. Scrooge felt that old familiar pang of helplessness, a relic of his past life when he'd ignorantly turned from suffering, not confronting it.

But now, defiantly brimming with newly kindled hope, he knelt beside his nephew, clasping his hand as if willing his own strength into the ailing man. His meager hopes dangled precariously upon the wisdom of those same physicians who had restored Tiny Tim to health and vibrancy.

"Uncle," Fred whispered, his voice scarcely stronger than a sigh, yet imbued with a warmth that could reach through the veil of even the severest illness. "You have come."

Even amidst the harsh illness cloaking him like a shroud, he exuded a courage and joy opposed to his current state of health; it was as though the embodiment of Christmas had taken refuge in him, defying the shadows threatening to encroach upon his spirit minute by minute.

"Of course, my boy," Scrooge replied, his throat tight with emotion, a myriad of feelings churning within him. "Of course, I would come when you needed me, and when you called out! What else would you imagine I might do, beloved boy? I tell you, I am here now and shall not leave your side. I have called for London's best medics, who ought to be able to get you back on your feet in no time."

He forced a smile, a mere shadow of his former self, masking the horrible uncertainty gnawing at him like a wretched spirit haunting the recesses of his heart. He placed his hand on Fred's forehead, feeling the burning heat radiating from his skin, a vicious reminder of the trial they were facing.

"You will be up and out of that sick bed very soon, my boy," Scrooge insisted.

Yet poor Fred's face looked so afraid. "Uncle, I ... No, Uncle, I am going away."

"Going away? Going where?" Scrooge nearly shouted the words.

"To the next place, Uncle. To ... wherever the dying go, after they pass. I cannot fight it."

His voice was so weakened, so awfully tremulous. So defeated, already halfway to the next plane.

"Cannot fight it? That is preposterous!" Scrooge was shouting at the top of his lungs. "But you must! Do you hear me? You must fight it! Otherwise, if you do not fight it, what do I have? Tell me! Tell me what I would have in this world if you were to leave me! No, I will not accept it!"

The young man in the sick bed looked sorely afraid, whiter than ever, stick-thin limbs growing cold.

Scrooge was aware of his voice being plaintive again, of him again focusing on his own introspective self. It was sinful. Young Fred had taught him that much.

He was supposed to be helping his nephew, not heaping blame and guilt on the boy's meager frame.

Selfish, that's what you are, Ebenezer Scrooge, his little inner voice reproached.

But he needed the boy. Wanted the boy. Loved the boy more than any words could tell!

And he just could not bear—

His thoughts shut off, his agonized psyche bringing down an unwilling gate of despair, shutting off his willingness to even contemplate such a thing as the boy not pulling through.

He swallowed the lump in his throat, feeling the stinging of his eyes, chest heaving.

Next, he turned away his head, avoiding any chance of Fred seeing the fat tears sliding down both cheeks. Then, out of nowhere, he surged forward onto the side of the bed, clutching at Fred's hand. "I forbid it. You hear me? I expressly forbid that you take it into your mind to go anyplace else!"

He shook his nephew's upper body with a tremendous force, hopefully shaking sense into him.

But still the lad's spirits could not be buoyed. Not now. His fight had all but departed, and the light was leaving his eyes. When he spoke, it was as a whisper of death, the words themselves chilled too.

"Do you remember, Uncle?" Fred murmured, bringing his beloved uncle a tiny bit closer by pulling on his hand. He wanted to be sure Scrooge could hear every word.

The final vestiges of light were igniting within Fred's fevered gaze. "Do you still remember those Christmases we spent together, you and I, bantering over the merits of turkey versus goose? Amusing, is it not? I recall it. Uncle, do you also recall your stubborn insistence on frugality even in the face of festivity? And look at you now. Never was a young man prouder of his uncle. Never …"

Scrooge chuckled softly, a sound tinged with nostalgia, even in these gravest of circumstances.

"Aye, you were a relentless one for merriment, Fred," Scrooge managed to muster, fighting the tremors, the hitch in his words. "More than once, I feared you might bring about the end of my quietude. But … it was worth it to see you happy. At least I am glad you approve of me now."

Fred squeezed his uncle's hand with an effort that seemed monumental given his weakened state. "And now, my dear uncle, it is your laughter I wish to hear once more. Mine has ceased but I had good times, very good. Do not turn away from joy, Uncle, even in the thick of sorrow such as you may be feeling today; embrace joy just the same way as you would carry on holding me …if able to."

Scrooge, moved beyond measure by the fortitude emanating from his nephew, felt grief stricken. "Rest now, Fred. As I said, I promise I shall be here, and when you rise again, oh, how we shall celebrate Christmas together! As it should be celebrated! The finest feast this city has ever known, with all the trimmings. I'll buy us the biggest turkey they've got in the butcher's shop, and there shall be no end to the multitude of corny carols your heart desires. I'll spare no expense in the celebration of another joyous season with my dear nephew. Now, boy, get off to sleep. And remember that I said I will not have you disappearing off to … to … that other place. Boy, do as I tell you."

Although Fred was a man by now, Scrooge still insisted on calling his nephew "boy." Somehow, it seemed to greatly solidify the bond between the two, and on occasions, Fred would return the gesture, calling out to his uncle, "Old man!" Then, Scrooge would pretend to be annoyed by it.

With a faint smile, Fred drifted briefly into a sleep sorely needed, and as Scrooge sat quietly by and watched over him, the churning tempest within him was beginning to settle.

Perhaps this moment of vulnerability was, at long last, a bridge to the joy he had long denied.

And the boy would, of course, be fine. He would keep telling himself this.

***

Days grew into nights, and Scrooge was still keeping vigil at the bedside, endlessly urging the doctors to do more, to try harder, to run more tests, draw more blood and infuse more water.

It was as if his desperate pleas might somehow summon wisdom from the heavens or ignite a spark of miraculous healing in Fred's frail and bony frame.

It was beyond belief that Fred, in the moments when his pale and watery eyes did manage to open, retained his positivity and humor, the tiniest light coming to his jaundiced eyes when he saw his uncle still sitting there each time. But the words he had spoken to his uncle were true. He tried now to make light of them, hoping to make his uncle laugh aloud, just to hear it for the last time.

"Uncle, I swear you are sitting here just to avoid work. You waster, you … you scoundrel!"

His uncle's lips would purse, but no joy came from them, no laughter.

"Of course, I will sit here for all the rest of my days if …"

There were no other words Scrooge could speak. His voice failed him.

Their eyes met, each brimming with water, both throats choked up. They held hands across the chilly bed covers, clutching one another as if nothing could ever seek to part them.

Fred was struggling, and no one could deny that he was growing far weaker day by day. He was holding on only because of Scrooge's refusal to allow him to go, a painful and intolerable suffering.

Now, when Scrooge tried to spoon porridge into Fred, his nephew could barely swallow it down.

When he flung open the dusty curtains to let in the light, Fred would shield his face, saying, "Uncle, the sunlight hurts so much. Please, close the curtains. Please don't let the daylight get to me."

The natural man was yearning for darkness, for that endless release, the final curtain of black.

Lately, there had even been days on which Scrooge had reached for his nephew's hand, only to want to pull away again. Fred's limbs were far too cold by now, and his hands had grown skinny.

Each hour dragged on, laden with yet more heartache, the flickering candlelight hurling mocking shadows, cruel reminders of a life once full of exuberance, now shrouded in a grim and suffocating hush. Despite the best efforts of esteemed physicians and the fervent prayers of family, everyone silently acknowledged Fred was succumbing, eager to slip quietly away.

And so it was that on that most blessed of all holy days, Christmas Day itself, that Fred, whose heart had once swelled with such boundless joy at its mere mention, breathed his last. Departing from this mortal coil, gone to that eternal realm where sorrow shall trouble him no more—leaving behind loved ones who remember him fondly in fleeting visions as one who was taken from us far too soon.

***

In the depths of his tear-stained sorrow, a curious vision presented itself to Scrooge, so profound that it nigh lifted the weight from his weary heart. In that fleeting moment, he beheld what seemed to be a splendid reunion, a joining together again of his dear nephew Fred with the cherished spirit of Scrooge's sister, the late departed Fan. How radiant and youthful she appeared, her countenance aglow with joy as she wrapped her arms around her beloved son in a fervent embrace. She laid kiss after kiss on his cheek, the embodiment of the happiness that had once filled the childhood home Scrooge knew.

She did not look like a ghost, not reminiscent of a hellish specter from another world.

No, Fan looked youthful and vibrant, her skin aglow, hair shining, her eyes sparkling. Even when she had been alive, it was doubtful she could have looked any healthier.

In short, death suited her.

As for Fred, he too had lost his sallow, sickly look, becoming once more that vital, cheeky and sprightly youth of the bygone days before he had even wed.

The boy looked so young, so impossibly perfect. So angelic, almost.

Scrooge wondered with a fluttering heart, were his eyes betraying him in this hour of lament?

Or was he really being granted a glimpse beyond the veil separating the living from the dead?

Whether vision or truth, this sight, this most poignant and endearing tableau of reunion bestowed upon him solace, a balm. It was nurturing to envisage these effervescent souls, the pair who had so often kindled warmth in the hearts of all those they touched, reawakening their bond in a realm beyond all bounds of earthly experience. The moment was impossible—and yet was realer than anything.

His momentary solace was as ephemeral as the morning mist, however. As was always prone to happen in life, Scrooge soon found himself ensnared once more in reality's grim hold.

The joyous visage that had briefly cast light throughout the corridors of Scrooge's despondent heart dissipated like smoke on the wind, leaving behind only the bitter chill of loss.

The truth bore down upon him, heavy and inexorable, a great stone weighing on a heart besieged by grief; the pang of realization struck him anew, piercing the lingering tendrils of hope, reminding him that his dear nephew was now but a whisper among the faint echoes of all that had gone.

Thus commenced a tempestuous journey of emotions, valleys darkened by a boundless greed festering in the heart of London, combining with this new and heartrending loss.

The boy had let him down. The boy had betrayed him, ignoring Scrooge's pleas for him to stay.

It was a blow so grievous it threatened to snuff out the flame of goodwill burning so brightly within Scrooge since his wondrous transformation. Yet, that renewed soul, a living emblem of benevolence and the embodiment of the glad season's happy spirit, would not be dimmed so easily.

If Scrooge allowed it to dissipate, then for what had Fred lived?

No! he would try to live in celebration of Fred's life, to be thankful!

Yes, Fred's passing had left a void so profound that no amount of trying could ever hope to fill it, a gaping chasm in Scrooge's heart now resonating with silence where laughter had thrived.

But this was the way of life, was it not? Just as he had admitted to himself, death came for all men, and sometimes, it came to claim them prematurely. Fred could never have fought it. He'd had no chance. Yet etched in his mind was the wondrous vision of Fred and Fan's joyous reunification, confirming that exodus from this mortal life and those left behind also meant grand gatherings of perfected souls, free from the pain and suffering rooted in this world.

Scrooge acknowledged that his own demands of God and the boy had been unreasonable. *Who am I to stand in the way of God's plan? We all must die to truly live it seems.*

Joy was all too fragile, his spirit burdened by the knowledge of how easily it could be swept away.

Scrooge mourned deeply, not only for Fred, his vibrant light extinguished far too soon, but also for the transitory nature of happiness; it was an elusive presence he had so diligently sought to cultivate these past years under Fred's tutelage. *Dear Fred. The one who was wiser than an old man like me ...*

Scrooge recalled all those cherished memories when Fred had persisted in building a relationship with his once ill-tempered uncle, their many moments of laughter, the warmth of Fred's unsolicited affection, the times when festivities had vibrated through the halls in symphony.

Now, he was left to grapple with the haunting truth that life, with all its capriciousness, could uplift the weary soul only to cast it down again, as cruelly as it had subdued it in the first place.

Scrooge often sat alone, shadows enveloping him again, the ghosts of his many regrets swirling with an insistent persistence. Grief was, at least, making him aware. Was that a bad thing?

One did not exist merely in the absence of grief; no, he could still flourish when embracing it fully, dark and light entwining in this fabric of being. Death was a vital part of life's meaning.

Yet still, those old enemies of times past—posing as friends—enveloped him anew with a suffocating intensity not known since that most harrowing visitation from the ghost of Christmas Yet to Come. Then, despair's shadows had frolicked menacingly before him, beckoning him to confront the chilling expectancy of his own mortality.

***

The days that followed were a blur.

Scrooge busied himself with the arrangements for Fred's funeral, ensuring no expense was spared to honor the man who had been like a son—or better than one—to him in all but name.

Each detail was meticulously planned, from the grand casket lined with soft velvet to the exquisite floral displays filling the church with a riot of color, reflecting the vibrant spirit Fred had embodied.

Scrooge pored over the arrangements, haunted by the memories of Fred's laughter, his passionate speeches, the infectious joy he had brought to those in his vicinity; these were all vital, unrelenting reminders of a warmth long neglected in his own self. In the quiet moments between tasks, regret was again refusing to let him settle. How much he had taken for granted! How very dismissive he had been toward all the good things in life, never counting his blessings. He'd had dear Fred, yet somehow, had still managed to regale everyone with talk of the mere miseries of life. It had never been true, for a life with Fred in it was surely beautiful. If only he had known it back then. If only he had been grateful.

The man he once had scorned had not only been family but also, Fred had shone a ray of light into his otherwise shadowy existence. Every heartfelt tribute burned in Scrooge, making him vow, "I will carry forward your legacy, dear Fred, determined to honor your memory and immeasurable greatness."

He would do justice to his nephew's unfulfilled potential, too.

The mourners, a veritable ocean of black-clad figures, were soon looking to Scrooge for comfort.

Alas, he was sure he had none to offer them, his sorrow having built into a chasm, vast and unbridgeable. "I know not what to say to you," he said to his fellow sufferers. "None could have loved Fred the way I did. None can possibly feel the void within me, the chasm he has left."

The last shovelful of earth now hurled on top of Fred's grave, Scrooge turned away, his steps leaden. The world around had dimmed, life's vibrant hues slain by such an immeasurable, boundless hurt.

He retreated to his home, seeking solace in solitude, and finding none.

***

In the weeks that followed, Scrooge's grief transformed. His work was far from over, and the legacy he hoped to leave was not one of fleeting gestures but of enduring improvement. Fred's children, the Cratchits, and countless others were looking to him not merely for gifts but also for guidance, for a vision of a world in which gentle compassion and goodness could triumph over greed.

As vibrant spring approached, he was intent on redoubling his efforts.

Yet even as he planned, an unease settled over him, as if the air itself carried a warning. Unbeknownst to him, his journey of mourning was as yet far from complete.

What was more, he would soon discover that the lessons he had learned would be tested in scarcely imaginable ways. For his legacy rested tediously on the precipice of failure, scarcely sustained by the branches forged by the ghosts of Christmases past, despite the recent steadiness provided by Fred's pull from beyond the veil. Redemption, fairness, yea the entirety of the human condition hanged in the balance against the rising tide of moral depravity in a world rapidly plunging toward tyranny and oppression.

In Memory of Fred

Chapter 2: Changing Times

London, once an emblem of quaint charm and measured industry, had swelled into a Leviathan of ceaseless frantic activity, growing larger and more unwieldy, a great beast rudely tugged from slumber.

A vibrant mosaic of humanity, London City vibrated with the fervor of ambition and, at times, echoed with the letting go of dreams stifled by the ever-grinding gears of an unfeeling machine.

The air—which, in days gone by had carried with it a brisk and invigorating freshness redolent of baked breads from warm hearths, the spice of merchants' wares, and soft musings of lovers promenading along tree-lined paths—now bore the acrid tang of soot, a prosaic testament to the agents of the relentless scourge called progress. A most vile, noxious breath arose from innumerable chimneys lining the city's sprawl, crudely belching forth plumes of dark smoke for which it never apologized.

These chimneys sent thick blackness rising ominously into the atmosphere, veiling the sun's gentle rays and dulling a once bright, azure expanse. This was the cause of the infamous London smog.

Gone were the days when the soundscape of London had been sweetened by the gentle chirps of birds or the tranquil stirrings of nature's bounty.

Now, the auditory miscellany had morphed into a cacophony of discordant notes.

London's melody was the gruffness of hammers striking iron, the clattering of carriage wheels over uneven cobbled streets, the brawling of drunks going at each other with broken bottles and slurs, and the ceaseless hum of machines creating an oppressive din intent on slaughtering man's hearing.

It was a symphony of hard labor punctuated by the anguished wails of children denied the light of play, gaunt faces and hopeless souls lost in adult burdens and relentless toil.

In this tempest of progress, Ebenezer Scrooge, who had tried to tread gaily and with a brisk step infused with purpose, felt like a leaf clinging desperately to a branch in the face of an unrelenting gale.

Though still revered as a benefactor to the poor, a guardian angel to those battered by life's cruel waves, he found himself increasingly isolated amid the swirling currents of a rapidly changing society.

In the heart of the city, its gilded interiors reflecting the ambitions of the upwardly mobile—those new magnates who rose like the sun after a prolonged, hard winter—it seemed that the spirit of charity he'd fought to instill in the citizens had become lost.

All that mattered these days was the relentless grind of profit margins and factory schedules.

His transformation from miser to generous benefactor, long admired and whispered about in taverns and parlors alike, had shaped the perceptions of many. To the impoverished, he was simply a saint, a herald of hope, whose warm-hearted deeds fostered gardens of growth in an arid, unfeeling desert.

But to the factory owners and industrial magnates, he had become a thorn in their side, an obstruction to their grand designs to reign with impunity, a stubborn remnant of a bygone era stupidly championing the whims of conscience over the priorities of making money and building even more factories for the future.

As London's elite gathered in their gleaming chambers—luxurious enclaves replete with fine silks and extravagant victuals—the phrase "Scrooge the Saint" escaped their lips with derision and incredulity. "His so-called philanthropy," they spat out, "emboldens the lower classes to dream beyond their station! It is a folly threatening to disrupt the finely tuned engine of progress and profit."

Their disdain oozed into the fabric of conversations, teeming with contempt for a man who would dare to lift the common worker's gaze above the dreary pavements they trod. They saw in him an enabler of insurrection, a rabble-rouser sowing discontent where gratitude should have flourished.

"Why should we accommodate the idle whims of the poor?" boomed Mr. Langston.

He was a portly merchant with a penchant for lavish balls and ostentatious displays.

The man was widely known for indulging in sumptuous banquets worthy of King Henry VIII, the richness of which would have fed a poor city slum family forty times over.

"Let them fend for themselves as we once did! Greedy beggars! Charity breeds dependency, I say! We all know that the only place for these vermin is in the workhouse."

Another gentleman's face, gaunt and wary, turned to Langston with hesitant eyes, quietly whispering, "But perhaps, my dear Langston, there is merit in Scrooge's way; he does command the respect of those he aids. Is it wise to antagonize one who holds such sway over the common man?"

"Fiddlesticks!" Langston waved his wine glass, irked. "Do you not see? Scrooge is but a moth fluttering about the flame of his own self-aggrandizing delusions! He strains to bind the wings of progress, all whilst cradling the masses like children, offering only the most superficial morsels. It serves no purpose but to weaken our resolve! Merit in his way? Poppycock! Besides, we can't have him rallying the pauper and rabble! It's a threat to our wealth, power, and social dominance."

Little did they realize that beneath the tumultuous surface, Ebenezer Scrooge, that once solitary titan of industry, had been irrevocably transformed. The icy tendrils of the loss of his nephew had awakened new depths in him, ceaseless past echoes whispering lessons few seemed willing to heed.

To Scrooge, each face passing by could reveal—with the simple light of a smile or the cascade of laughter—the same brilliance of humanity that Fred had possessed. He was fiercely committed to immortalizing Fred's legacy and spreading abroad the delight Fred so wanted the discarded working class to enjoy. Yet as he observed, the shadows cast by greed and disconnection still came creeping through the dark doorways of society.

The night persisted in coming to oppress the light, an ugly phenomenon happening daily, right before his eyes. *Perhaps, then,* he mused, *I must offer free lamps to all those who would herald and hail the dark, such that they may experience how it is to live in the vivid brightness of my Fred's world.*

I cannot drag them kicking and screaming into more benevolent ways, can I?

That would be a folly.

But I can coax them, lead them like a dog to the water bowl. Gently, gently ...

Pragmatic as he had become in his old age, Scrooge discerned that to cater to hope was not to stifle ambition, but rather to cultivate a green pasture, a place for all to ultimately flourish.

And thus, in this hallowed ground of unassailable ambition, he wrapped his cloak tighter against his body in the chill of the biting London air, understanding that wearisome battles awaited.

I am willing to endure the battle for the soul of a city straining under the yoke of its own creation, eager for its wealth and newfound glitter, he thought. Scrooge resolved to guard, like a sentinel of old, the spark of compassion in the eyes of laborers, the future dreams of waifs scuttling through alleyways, and the hope of weary hearts longing to be valued in a world already burying their names.

Ambling through these increasingly meddlesome city streets, he found himself haunted by reminders of Fred, but not in a bad and irksome way, more like an eager child, urging him on.

Had those vile ghosts of Christmases Past become replaced by Fred's glad specter hounding him?

Doggedly and yet in joy, the spirit seemed to follow on his heels to ensure he carried out his promises, not just letting ambition die as he'd know the old Scrooge would have done.

It seemed that Fred was determined for Scrooge to see him everywhere!

Fred's memory, his laughter and zest for life were dancing like phantoms in the frigid air, teasing him in the swirling shadows, each turn in alleyways unfurling a weave of bittersweet memories.

There was the quaint coffeehouse, its windows aglow with candle flames, the place where he and Fred had shared countless cups of steaming cocoa during the winter holidays.

The rich aroma mingled with laughter and warmth, reminiscent of their glee.

The dancing street lamps beckoned to him, reminding him of the twinkle in Fred's eyes, bright orbs filled with unquenchable spirit and childlike wonder. Amidst this gentle reverie emerged the heart-wrenching contradiction of the poor and destitute, the ones so many eyes were refusing to see, even when their feet stumbled over them in the gutter as they lay huddled in ragged heaps to keep warm.

Their hollow eyes beseeched for scraps of kindness, poignant reminders of Fred's generous nature, for he would have willingly surrendered his last penny to ease the suffering of the less fortunate.

Now, the bricks of old familiar places were whispering harsh truths, cheerful façades dulled by the relentless march of time and progress.

Wasn't it ignorant and meaningless to be human when humanity had morphed into avaricious greed? Time—in which to drive progress—was carelessly slipping through his fingers.

He was oftentimes becoming a prisoner of his own sorrow, wandering aimlessly through clouds of melancholy, his mind spiraling down, entangling itself in the innumerable crevices of self-pity.

Only when the chiming of the clock struck the solemn hour of nine, sonorously resonating through the fray of his thoughts, did he startlingly find himself standing alone at the threshold to his office.

Indeed, he had latterly become an uninvited visitor to a place that felt increasingly like a mausoleum rather than a sanctuary, its warmth and welcome dim and distant in the wake of so much tumult.

Here, the last vestiges of joy had become replaced by solitude's oppressive weight.

The small voice inside Scrooge kept telling him, *but sir, the only way to uplift oneself, and to uplift all of*

mankind, is to give, to make, to honor, to create,
to worship, to be merciful and bountiful ...

"Yes, yes, I hear you!" he cried impatiently. "That's all very well but tell me what to do! All you ever do is tell me how things are not enough! How I am hopeless and failing in my task! How I think only introspectively, delighting again in my misery. So just ... for goodness' sake, tell me what to do to get there, to that place of light. The place to which I promised Fred I would lead the poor and the downtrodden, the destitute. The truth is, I've no idea how."

Ashamed and cowed, Scrooge scurried his way into his modest office, forcing himself to focus on the business of the day. His work could never free him from his melancholy, though he feigned that it might. He wandered to reviewing letters of appeal from charitable societies, missives painting the grimmest picture: families displaced by factory expansion; children maimed and slaughtered, eviscerated by machinery; neighborhoods swallowed by the relentless march of ruthlessness.

He sighed deeply, his hand resting on a letter from a widow.

'Please, sir, we have all heard how good you are
to the poor.

Please help me to pay my son's burial fees; only
eleven years old, he succumbed to a fever contracted in
the fetid confines of the workhouse. May the Lord grant
him eternal peace.

I shall await hearing news from you, and may
God bless you for all the good that you do.

In faith and tears,

Minnie Copthorne.'

"What have we gained," he murmured to himself, "if progress comes at the cost of our humanity?"

As if summoned by his lamentation, the door creaked open, and Lily—Fred's widow and Scrooge's partner in benevolence—entered.

Her face, though warm with the glow of purpose, also bore lines since Fred's passing. "Another evening of grim tidings, Ebenezer?" she asked, setting down a ledger.

"Indeed, Lily," Scrooge replied, resigned. "It seems the more we give, the less it suffices. For every family we aid, ten more fall into despair. They crumble around us, becoming as dust."

Lily's expression softened as she laid a hand on his shoulder.

"Do not lose heart, Uncle. Your kindness inspires, and your example—though contested by the few —has sparked hope among many. Fred would not want you to overlook what good you perform."

Before Scrooge could respond, a knock interrupted. A young clerk entered, bearing yet another letter, this one sealed with an imposing crest.

The wax bore the mark of the London Industrial Association, a powerful consortium of businessmen wielding significant influence over the city's policies.

Scrooge's brows knitted as he broke the seal and read the contents.

The letter was direct and cold.

> 'To Mr. Ebenezer Scrooge,
>
> *We find it necessary to address a matter of utmost importance regarding your recent*

purportedly 'philanthropic' undertakings. While your intentions may seem noble at first glance, they give rise to an unfortunate vulnerability among the working classes, a vulnerability that now threatens the foundations upon which society rests.

We implore you to reassess the breadth of your efforts, for in attempting to alleviate the plight of the uneducated and downtrodden, you unwittingly stifle the industrious spirit fueling our city's necessary progress. Remember, true advancement often demands sacrifices, and allowing sentimentality to cloud one's better judgment is a perilous misstep obstructing the wheels of innovation we hold so dear for our children's futures.

We request a written reply without delay.

Yours with the utmost concern,
The London Industrial Association.'

Scrooge's face flushed with indignation and his shoulders slumped.

"For our children's futures, indeed! What tosh! In what world do they reside when they think that belching, acrid smoke is the way to ensure a young man will thrive? Sacrifice, they say! And whose sacrifice do they demand? Not their own, for sure. No, as always, it is the poor who are to bear the brunt, while they count their gold and build towering empires on the backs of the subjugated commoners. If only they could have visits from ghostly apparitions, then they might see the error of their ways as I did."

Lily's eyes narrowed imperceptibly, tenderness and resolve combining.

She cradled Scrooge's head gently within her hands, lifting it so that he might meet her gaze. Her own eyes searched his with an intensity piercing the veil of his troubled heart.

"There is moisture in your eyes, Uncle," she began. "It sits in mine too, but what you must do is obvious," she declared. "Do you not see it? They fear you, Ebenezer. Your example reveals their greed for what it is. They fear being exposed; that is why they seek to silence you. Bands of warriors do not rise up against one man. They rise against a throng posing a threat to their way of life."

He did not understand. "I am just one man," he argued. "I am sure they hardly feel put upon."

She put her finger to his lips. "Hush. You are beyond one man. You have become the throng they fear. Can you not see? Can you not grasp why they fear you getting your way? You are what unsettles them. You are a nightmare rising them in the dark, their worst fear. This is why they seek to stop you."

"Let them try," Scrooge declared, rising from his chair with renewed fire. "I will not stand by while the city I love becomes consumed by this … this ungodliness! If they see my compassion as weakness, then so be it. But I will continue to fight for those who lack a voice, the ones with no power."

The resolve in Scrooge's voice lent Lily a flicker of brief smile.

***

As Scrooge himself had voiced, he was but one man—a solitary speck upon the boundless main—with a seemingly insurmountable duty. As days inexorably stretched into weeks, the sinister influence of the London Industrial Association only loomed larger.

It was casting black shade over his every endeavor.

Their campaign to undermine him commenced with a fervor that could only be likened to the insidious machinations of a serpent in the grass.

Whispers came slithering through the city, rumors darting like birds startled from their nests, proclaiming that Scrooge's charities were disordered heaps of mismanagement in gilded wrappings.

His benevolent efforts, they said, were fostering a culture of indolence, and that he stood, a hapless onlooker, entirely out of touch with the bustling realities of a modern economy.

"He is a buffoon!" they said in the papers. "Such an idiot lives among us."

How rich was their hypocrisy!

Here, these architects of rapacity, themselves accumulating dirty wealth at an alarming rate, spoke with such lofty disdain, all while lining their pockets with coin derived from the labors of the afflicted.

In a world where golden coins clinked louder than the cries of the needy, they hurled accusations, not to explain or apologize, merely to justify their shameful pursuits.

Regardless, Scrooge, in his earnestness, still sought to uplift the downtrodden. But this was war, and Scrooge had never anticipated the strength of the army against whom he fought.

There would be hard times to come because of this, bitter and lean times.

In the once-thriving domain of Scrooge's business ventures, the winds of fortune began to shift ominously, casting the formerly rosy glow of prosperity into shadow. Contracts, once eagerly clasped in the firm grasp of mutual benefit, were abruptly withdrawn, and partnerships—sacred bonds of commerce—were insidiously cleaved asunder as if by the swift hand of some merciless henchman.

His coffers, previously emanating the harmonious clink of success, were being plundered, drained relentlessly and systematically by his endeavors to lift the downtrodden people who dared not breathe.

Yet, amid this gathering tempest, and although the nefarious London Industrial Association wielded influence like a blunt instrument with which to bludgeon him, threatening those who dared associate with him or engage in his noble contracts, Scrooge stood resolute.

"My integrity is of utmost importance! I shall not let covetous fools such as this derail me from my divinely appointed course," he mused quietly.

If they slaughtered him, so be it. Every man died sometime, did he not?

He would rather die in the pursuit of a noble venture than wither from a lack of purpose and surrender to the tides of apathy.

He continued to give with a generosity belying his diminishing coffers, advocating passionately for the downtrodden, illuminating the way toward a brighter future for the impoverished masses.

One evening, as Scrooge walked home through the bustling streets, he paused to observe a group of factory workers emerging from their labors. Their faces were ashen with fatigue, their hands calloused and worn. Among them was a boy no older than twelve, his small frame bowed under the weight of a humongous stuffed coal sack. The sight evoked vivid memories of a cherished love long past, for Scrooge could not help but recall the days when his dear sister, Fan, would toil diligently beneath the stern gaze of their father, but she had carried on with a quiet strength, indomitable.

Those languid hours spent laboring, unseen and unappreciated, under the watchful scrutiny of an unforgiving parental eye, had lit in him a profound empathy for her struggles.

How she had labored with a tenacity veiling her tender years, striving to carve out warmth and joy amidst the stark and callous realities of their upbringing! Such recollections kindled a rush of nostalgia, intertwining the marrow of his memories with the realization that the fires of resilience burned brightly in those he adored, just as they had in his own fragile youth.

Scrooge approached the boy and gently lifted the sack, relieving him of his burden.

"What is your name, lad?" he asked.

"Tom, sir. Really, Thomas, but I like Tom better," the boy replied, his voice barely above a whisper, and his eyes fixed to the ground as if God would smite him dead if he dared to look up.

"Tom, do you know what day it is?"

The poor lad could hardly get a word out without becoming breathless.

"Tuesday, sir."

Scrooge smiled faintly. "No, my boy. It is the first day of your new life. Now, come with me and let us see what can be done to improve things for you. You need not lug coal anymore."

That fateful night, under the dim glow of gas lamps in the encroaching darkness, Scrooge's newfound determination commenced its path through aged veins, orchestrated a series of events to alter the course of young Tom's life. He could not help all the poor people. He could not give succor to everyone who was starving. But he could start small, helping one at a time, beginning with Tom. Afterall, a solitary spark of fire could ignite a raging inferno.

With a heart brimming with unexpected warmth, he set about securing better lodgings for Tom and his family, a modest yet sturdy dwelling to shelter them from the biting chill.

Each move he made, each detail to which he attended, resonated with intensity, as though he were not merely aiding a struggling family, but also nurturing a future.

He could envision it unfurling, rich with promise.

In his pursuit to elevate the boy's circumstances, Scrooge duly arranged for Tom to be admitted into the local school, a hallowed institution where the light of learning would soon replace the drudgery of factory toil. In this society, only the privileged could afford to still attend school at Tom's age.

Scrooge would ensure the boy became one of the privileged.

Calling in old favors with those still inclined to repay him, Scrooge ensured that the boy's education would come at no cost, removing yet another burden from the lad's weary shoulders.

No longer would the boy be a cog in industry's unforgiving wheels, but instead he would find himself enveloped in a world of knowledge, creativity, and possibility. The thought of this transformation filled Scrooge with a sense of connection. It almost felt as though Tom were a son who fortune had denied him in his life, a surrogate embodiment of what might have been.

Of course, the youngster had his own family, but nothing stopped Scrooge treating him like the lost son he had never had. And in many ways, the boy also reminded him a little of darling Fred.

With each passing moment, envisioning Tom donning a school cap and traversing the halls of academia, reminiscences of Scrooge's childhood—for which he was regretful—reared their heads.

The small act of kindness he could bestow on the boy, a trifling act amid the vast sea of despair plaguing London, served as a poignant reminder that individual lives could be transformed through tenderness. External pressures bore no real influence when the inner was strong.

Scrooge felt moved, bathed in a palpable bloom of fire; he had not only changed a boy's destiny. He had rekindled a sense of purpose in his own beleaguered soul.

Amidst the 'pea soup' fog of London's night, he recognized that love—of blood or spirit—could transcend the hardest of beginnings.

Still, as Scrooge lay in bed that night, his thoughts turned to the larger battle.

The forces arrayed against him were formidable; how could he ignore the growing sense that his solitary efforts, however noble, might not suffice to stem this tide of grasping indifference?

"What more can I do?" he wondered aloud. "How can one man even hope to change the course of a city so consumed by its own greedy ambition? I surely deceive myself with a task so immense."

As sleep overtook, he settled into dreaming of a vast, shadowy figure standing at the edge of the city, a mighty outstretched hand beckoning.

"Come, come," it whispered, gesturing. "Come to the city! We need you here …"

In its other hand, it held out a lantern, casting a pale light to pierce the darkest blackness. Though he could not discern its face, there seemed to be a peculiar familiarity and foreboding.

In his past when he'd been on the other side, the bad side, he had never seen for himself that the blackness was more than one shade. Now, he saw there were many hues of it. And the writing pit of vipers, industry's cruel strangulation of all that was good, this was the blackest of them all.

***

When Scrooge awoke, the dream was lingering.

Though he could not yet comprehend its meaning, he resolved to press on regardless, guided by the belief that even in the darkest times, a single candlelight could issue its glow into the universe.

Chapter 3: The Shadow of Loss

Spring, with its tender cherry blossoms and gentle breezes, had long since passed. So too had the sweetest summer, the golden hues of which had lingered only to give way in the end.

Now, it was the turn of autumn's crisp embrace, soon to turn to another icy-tendrilled winter.

The cool air was already thick with the scent of damp leaves and the acrid bite of coal smoke, oppressive dense air hanging over the city. On the very coldest nights, when people raced home to stoke their fires and pull warm blankets around their children, the infamous London smog would descend over everything. They call it a 'pea souper' since it was pungent and acrid, the smoke from the belching chimneys being forced to the ground by the city's polluted air.

It was on this evening, with the wind biting sharply, that Ebenezer Scrooge bore a chill far deeper and more unforgiving than usual. He was feeling unusually burdened.

These days, he was trying to turn over a new leaf, attempting to view the world through happier eyes. Indeed, dispelled were the days of complaining and griping, moaning and whining.

Well, supposedly.

It had been weeks since Scrooge had last enjoyed the companionship of Lily, Fred's cherished widow, and their lively, noisy brood. This was odd in itself, since when Fred had been alive, Uncle Scrooge had been a regular visitor, bringing gaiety and cheer to their dinner table.

The fleeting moments he had lately shared with them had each been marred by the dreariness of business, absent of the warmth and joy once coloring their exchanges. How his heart ached for the laughter and light to fill this home again, now eclipsed by the cumbersome shadows of his making!

Each second of flickering candlelight seemed to only highlight how murky the darkness really was.

With the bells of St. Paul's Cathedral tolling solemnity in the evening's dampness and gloom, Scrooge's worst fear was making a reappearance, coming back tenfold.

With the great bells' tolling, there seemed to come the harbinger of death itself, crying out, "Hark ye all, death and doom be soon upon ye! All efforts are in vain! Death calls, death calls …"

It was as if the universe conspired to remind him of the joy that had slipped through his fingers, leaving behind a void so profound that nothing could ever hope to fill it.

As the rebirth of grief settled in his heart, he understood the true cost of his silence, the heavy toll of love unspoken and companionship forsaken.

Grief, that most treacherous of emotions, was known to move through the human spirit like restless sea tides, surging and receding with an unpredictable rhythm defying comprehension.

It seemed to ebb away, bringing a smile.

Then without warning, it would surge again, tearing everything with it, all new life drowned.

He was crying often, and hard, when alone. In these unwelcome moments—the recollections of Fred's joyous laughter echoing in the hall, or when Scrooge remembered the affectionate light in his nephew's eyes during festive gatherings—that pain's weight became overwhelming.

This time, it almost defeated him, tugging him under.

As with many destined to suffer fate's cruel hand, Scrooge was only just discovering that grief did not diminish with time's onslaught; like a chameleon, it learned to assume fresh forms.

There were days when he moved through the world cloaked in the frigid armor of disdain, fighting his attempts to bury the deep-seated sorrow beneath layers of cynical bitterness.

Then would come those giant waves of despair, uninvited and merciless, crashing over him.

He was thinking of Fred, remembering Fred. Desperately needing Fred. Being angry at Fred. Sometimes, even hating God, who he blamed for ripping such a young person away.

It happened most often whenever he saw a family gathered around a table, laughter ringing out.

It felt as though the foundation upon which he stood threatened to crumble, misery conspiring to claw at his insides until he had been disemboweled by inner torment.

The doom-laden reminder came to again press home the message that however hard he toiled at the new venture, however much he lifted himself via benevolent and altruistic deeds, loss could always shatter the heart anew. It did not even matter how many seasons had drifted by.

Such were the capricious ways of grief, a seemingly dormant ember that could ignite without warning, engulfing him in waves of yearning.

It was in that moment of desperation whispering through barren, dejected loneliness that Scrooge felt an undeniable urge to seek out Fred's widow.

Was not Lily the woman whose spirit had once danced with the warmth of Fred's love?

Was she not the same woman whose heart now toggled between sorrow and remembrance, just as his own was doing? A pang of shame gripped him for having neglected her and her family for weeks.

In his absence, he had allowed selfishness to encroach on the light of their connection.

How could he overlook them? How deceptively superficial was he if he could just let her go?

Perhaps, Scrooge mused, in the timorous querying of his wretched psyche, Lily might be a touchstone, a willing, shiny anchor in the tumultuous waters battering at his weary mind.

He should not forget that poor Lily, with all her youth, her graceful poise and gentle strength, had borne witness to love's deepest joys, yet also the sharpest sorrows in also losing dear Fred.

Scrooge wondered, *what solace might be found in an exchange of our weariness?*

It was altogether unexpected, this impulse to reunite with the shadow of his nephew's life.

Ultimately, he'd only deprived himself of the cherished memories that might have been.

Yet, as the prospect of reuniting tugged at him with an almost supernatural insistence, Scrooge found himself rooted in uncertainty.

Could he even bear to confront the spirit of Fred through the delicate lens of Lily's mournful gaze? Perhaps one reason for avoiding her was that through her eyes, he swore he could still see Fred—and at times, as sad as he was, he needed to move on and forget him as best he could. The more he visited Lily, the more they spoke of their loss, the greater the turmoil.

It would all begin again. Wouldn't it?

It had been an eternity since he'd allowed himself the privy pleasure of an audience with her. So, maybe that was the reason for it, that it was a man's nature to want to get on with life. But did he need to shut her out totally? Was that not harking back to the same kind of callousness he'd shed?

But after so long, was it unreasonable and improbable to renew contact?

Would she think him foolish? A stupid old man, wallowing in his own self-pity?

Time, that relentless thief, had conspired to stretch the interval between their meetings into a chasm far too wide for comfort, and in this span, he had allowed himself to drift from her, bit by bit.

The longer the absence and the silence he invited between them, the more awkward and challenging it became to get back in touch. What would he say? How could he explain himself?

After all, as Fred's fondest uncle, was he not supposed to care for Lily almost as his own daughter?

He had let her down, and in doing so, he had let down his nephew, his nephew's wife, and their beloved children—the offspring of dear Fred! He was mortified, also acknowledging that at the same time as he'd been shunning Lily and the children, he had been pouring focus and time into young Tom, someone he had barely even met before removing him from the coal drudgery.

No, he had to go and make his apologies, right now!

Well, perhaps not right now. Later.

The truth was, he could not bring himself to face them free of fear.

He wished to be nearer to her, to ensure she was well and looking after herself and the children—yet at the same time, he wanted nothing more than to flee, to hide from their sorrow-cast miens.

To encounter Lily was to confront the preternatural apparition of Fred, a haunting reminder of the joy now extinguished, leaving behind only its haunting resonance.

This bittersweet association prevailed upon him, urging him to retreat into the uninviting recesses of his mind. Isolation offered a wretched form of comfort.

Alas, the hideousness of that sentiment, self-pity!

No wonder wiser men pitied the fools who lost themselves in it!

He should have known better. And even if he had not known better, he should at the very least have recognized that wallowing in 'poor me' could not offer a way to save him from himself.

Scrooge pondered on things gravely, looking through the frost-clad windowpane, witnessing the world outside bustling with life, everyone celebrating and sharing love.

To seek out Lily would require more than mere words; it would demand vulnerability, a willingness to embrace both his own frailty and the grief that may still appear.

There, in that dimly lit room, Scrooge resolved to step beyond desolation's threshold.

The connection, however tenuous, might weave a thin and tenuous thread of warmth through the frigid latticework of his existence. With this in mind, he made a promise.

"I need to visit her," he voiced quietly. "I need to see Lily … before it becomes too late."

***

A pallid twilight settling over the cobbled London streets, shadows stretched their bony fingers of remorse and Ebenezer Scrooge found himself adrift in a sea of trepidation.

With each hesitant step, the resolute drumming of his heartbeat resounded against crisp autumn air, a constant rapping of the beat of much squandered time.

This should have been simple.

It should have been easy enough to put one black-booted foot in front of the other until he reached her door, yet the farther he walked, the slower his steps. He was neither weary nor lost; he was anxious and afraid that she would not appreciate him visiting like this anymore.

The path that had brought him closer to her home seemed to be conspiring against him now, stretching like the endless corridors of memory. Time itself appeared to be dissipating into the ether, unnoticed. The world around was fading into an indistinct murmur: the laughter of children playing in the distance; the creaking of nearby shutters; the soft chirping of sparrows settling for the night.

These all mingled into a symphony of forgotten, unlikely joy. Scrooge, wrapped in a cloak of apprehension, marched onward anyway, aware that this fleeting yet monumental hour had the power to reshape the contours of his existence for good or ill if only he possessed the fortitude to embrace it.

Finally, the door loomed ahead at the top of the lamp-lined stony street, the fog settling.

With a resolute breath that seemed to draw from the depths of his being, Scrooge raised his knotted hand and rapped on the door, each knock sending a frisson of anxiety down his body.

Had he rapped too hard? Could it have frightened them? Maybe she wouldn't come to the door.

Yet the house still seemed welcoming, humble yet vibrant, issuing reminders of a life well-lived.

There was the familiar scent of baked bread and distant laughter.

Soon enough, there came a light-footed *skip-skip* of dainty feet wending toward him down the inner hallway, then a small voice begging, "I am coming. I must fetch a lamp; please, be patient, stranger."

When the door eventually swung open, revealing Lily with her radiant smile and bright, welcoming eyes, an overwhelming radiance enveloped him. "Oh! Not a stranger! Uncle!" she gasped, delighted.

She was standing in the doorway with a small brass lamp in her hand, holding it up to light the visitor's face. Upon recognizing him, she chuckled and stepped forward, arms outstretched.

"Oh, Ebenezer!" she exclaimed, her voice a melodic balm to his troubled self.

She clasped him tightly, eyes glistening with a sudden, tender moisture, transforming his trepidation into a rapture he had long believed beyond reach. Clasping his hand, she enthused, "You know, I've been praying you'd come."

In that singular moment, the world around melted away. He was a man reborn.

As they stood wrapped in that unspeakably beautiful moment, Scrooge felt the burden of weeks spent in solitary disdain lifting as he took a step back to look into Lily's eyes.

Her embrace had ignited something long-extinguished in him, remorse for the distance he had created, both between the family of Fred and within himself.

He was almost rendered wordless by his humility and gracious welcoming.

"I have been such a fool, Lily," he began, his voice quivering with the sincerity of long-held regrets. "In my stinginess and my fears, I ... I cast aside all the greatest treasures of my life, forgetting that joy flourishes in the bond of family and the laughter of these children. Please, forgive me."

She seemed not to know what to say, just holding him at arm's length, grinning.

With her brow furrowed in concern yet softened with comprehension, Lily listened intently as he continued, "I vow to you, and to our precious children"—for Scrooge had vowed to become a father figure to Fred's children, thinking of them as his own—"that I will no longer be a specter haunting these halls. No longer will I trade warmth for fleeting shadows! I wish to be present, to share in your joys, to be a father to those little ones who deserve a man full of life, a man who revels in the beauty of every brief moment. Though I know I can never replace Fred as their father, I am determined to embrace them with all the love and guidance they need, to be a steadfast presence, nurturing them as only a devoted guardian can. Please, Lily, may I fulfill my duty to you and them?"

He had spoken so much—and so fast—that he was nearly breathless.

He rested a hand on the wall as if he would fall over otherwise. And perhaps he would because in horror, he realized it may have sounded like a marriage proposal from a man three times her age!

"I-I don't know what I said there. I just wish to do my best for you all. No greater motive."

He was shivering.

They both became aware he was still standing on the doorstep, dampness in his hair and whiskers.

Her gaze filling with both surprise and delight, she nodded, the corners of her mouth lifting as though Scrooge had breathed new life into their shared history.

"I know there is no motive, silly. Don't be so foolish, my dear Uncle," she said, laughing lightly, taking hold of his hand. "You are so *silly* for even thinking I could assume so. I know you, Ebenezer Scrooge, and you are a good man."

They found their way to a pact forged not merely in words, but also in the unyielding bond of platonic, deep love held steadfast.

The family had been waiting patiently for the day when Scrooge would finally come around.

"Anyway, you must be freezing out here, Ebenezer," she said gently, stepping back to open the door wider, inviting him into the warmth of their little sanctuary with a wave of her hand.

"I gave quite a desperate little speech on the threshold of your house," he said sheepishly. "Yes, I am indeed freezing. A cup of your finest tea would not go amiss if you can bear to entertain me, the ridiculous old fool that I have become in your eyes."

He chuckled, and she joined in, gently pulling him into the hallway. "A fool indeed," she said. "But some people love an old fool. I have never been gladder to see anyone on my step."

He grinned. "Truly?"

"Come! Come inside!" Her hand wafted again. "The children will be thrilled to see you, and there's a pot of stew on the fire. And there is always tea for you, and fresh bread. You need to warm yourself, not just from the cold, but from the long shadows in which you have been wandering. Or hiding."

Her voice, enriched with kindness, sang.

Every fiber of his being was alight with singing too. As he crossed the threshold and stepped into the inviting glow of the hearth, the barriers he had erected were all deconstructing.

And it felt good. No—it felt beyond perfect, amazing, miraculous … all those things.

He had almost forgotten how beautiful it was to be a part of something so wonderful: a family.

As they settled into the comfortable parlor, the gentle crackle of the fire filled the air.

Lily poured them both a cup of steaming tea, the rich aroma curling upward as tendrils of steam rose, mingling with the heady and deep aroma of woodsmoke.

Scrooge glanced around, taking in the cozy décor.

The handmade trinkets from their children, the faint laughter resonating from the other room.

It offered such a stark contrast to the cold, lonely office and the increasing isolation to which he had grown accustomed of late. And, of course, he was gladdened to have been reunited with Lily.

Lily, her eyes red and swollen, gently touched Scrooge's shoulder, recognizing the guilt he must have been feeling. Her voice was hushed now, full of compassionate notes.

"Ebenezer, you were so strong for him, you know. You did everything you could possibly do. To allow yourself the freedom to grieve is—"

"Grieve?" Scrooge's voice was aghast, hollow, his gaze fixed on the image of Fred's pale face, looking at him from a framed picture atop a highly polished dark wood cabinet.

He had not come to this home to grieve!

No, he had come to help them both—to help them all—to move on!

He'd visited with a mind to learn to laugh again, to be happy, to join in with life! He had come here to help these beautiful children toward a better, more wholesome, joyous future. Not to grieve.

The grieving had to be done, over, gone. Because within it, he had been drowning, suffocating.

Now that she had brought up the topic of sorrow, it was flooding back. He was bereft.

"Lily, I beseech you to tell me, how does one grieve when the kernel of one's existence has been torn away? Tell me, Lily, what solace is there when joy itself chooses to depart the earth?"

Lily knelt beside him, her tears flowing freely, hopelessly clutching at his flailing hand.

What Scrooge did not know was that if he had allowed her to finish what she was saying, he would have heard her urging him to move on. That he was—they were—allowed to do so.

Those were the words she'd been about to speak.

His change in mood seemed to have caught her off guard; he almost seemed annoyed.

Finally, she said shyly, "Ebenezer, there is solace in remembrance, you know, in carrying forward the love he gave us. Fred would not wish for us to be lost in despair. Not forever, not like this."

Well, no, I know that, he thought, but he kept his ruminations to himself. *I was not any longer in despair when I set out to come here. The sun was beginning to glint through the trees, you know ...*

I was going to lift your world, to lighten the burden, to try to forge a path ahead for all of us.

But now, you have reminded me.

I miss our darling Fred so much. I cannot even bear it.

Why did you have to speak of grief?

He wanted to be alone again, to run away and find a quiet place, a sad place, and weep.

She paused, her gaze lifting to the cozy all-encompassing lit hearth.

"Ebenezer, in honoring our beloved Fred through the embrace of the spirit of Christmas all year long, we weave his legacy into the fabric of our lives, allowing joy to take root where sorrow once flourished, transforming our grief into a celebration of all that he was and still remains within us. What I was attempting to convey is we ought to be happy, Ebenezer, allowing ourselves pleasure and joy."

He was overcome with relief. And gladness! Lily, too, had been longing to find the light!

Scrooge's despair, a monstrous, chilling beast that had long held him captive, began to show again the first faint beams of celestial light, a nascent hope piercing the impenetrable gloom so long enshrouding his soul. And as this fragile spark of hope began to burgeon in Lily's kindness.

Scrooge had always seen Fred as a young man, steadfast and resolute in his optimism, his mirth unwavering even as Scrooge, in his own obstinate folly, had cast aside Fred's Christmas dinner invitations like fallen leaves on the winter ground, year after year.

Now, Scrooge saw Fred transformed.

Now, Fred was a loving husband and devoted father, standing as a mighty pillar of strength for his family; aglow, he had enhanced the lives of all who crossed his threshold. No wonder Lily no longer permitted herself to mourn. Fred would never have supported it. He had been a smiler, not a weeper.

As these cherished memories flitted as though real in his mind, Scrooge couldn't suppress a deep-seated longing to once more hear the brilliant orator Fred had become.

A veritable master of words and emotions, Fred's eloquence had been capable of igniting gaiety and raucous cheer in the most hardened of hearts.

In bittersweet reflection, Scrooge recalled the day when he had once quipped to Fred, "I wonder you don't go into Parliament," marveling at the young man's remarkable oratory gift.

He'd possessed a power that could rally and unite people.

"You really could, you know, Fred. You could become a marvelous politician."

The young man had instantly dismissed the usefulness of having such a talent, leaving only laughter in the wake of the suggestion, much to his uncle's profound chagrin and some embarrassment.

"Uncle," he had quipped, falling about himself with laughing. "You are the funniest man!"

***

Scrooge visited Lily and the children frequently after that, relishing being a part of their little tight-knit family. Sometimes, Lily and the children would get an early night, and Scrooge would sit by the fire, staring into the flames as if seeking answers within the oranges and yellows leaping high.

He would leave in the early light when the household awoke again, often making tea and porridge for when they stirred. Slowly but surely, life was improving but he needed to get back to the man who had vowed to make a difference. His transformation seemed unfinished.

What good is charity, he wondered, *when even the most generous heart cannot shield a loved one from life's cruelty? What is the value of redemption if it leaves one vulnerable to profound sorrow?*

Facing dawn anew, he committed himself to a broader mission; he would continue to seek out solutions to combat the avarice plaguing society and eroding the bonds of kinship and community.

He was back on track.

With newfound conviction, Scrooge vowed to act, not just to elevate his own heart but also to lift others from the grip of despair. The destitute. The sick. The afflicted. He would aid them all!

In honoring his beloved Fred, he would also be reclaiming humanity, one act of kindness at a time.

In the morning, he would talk with Lily, and he would come up with something.

Just then, as the remnants of Fred's laughter ebbed and flowed in the caverns of his mind, Scrooge found himself seized by a sudden recollection.

Hmm, that small wooden box that Lily bestowed upon me during our last bittersweet meeting ...

He had not even looked at it yet.

Its unassuming exterior, worn smooth by time and tender hands, beckoned to him.

It was an allure that transcended mere memory.

Compelled by a force he could not begin to name, Scrooge rose from his brooding contemplations to gently draw the little box from its resting place atop the mantle, determined to unveil its secrets.

As the snow fell softly outside, Scrooge opened this cherished wooden box that had belonged to Fred. Inside were letters, photographs, and trinkets, tokens of a life lived fully, in limitless love.

Of particular note, Scrooge, with a tremor in his hand, delicately lifted and examined a hand-carved Christmas tree ornament, a masterpiece of delicate artistry depicting the infant Jesus slumbering within a manger. The intricately carved wood, cool to the touch, seemed to whisper tales of forgotten Christmases, of laughter and merriment shared with his nephew.

Hidden at the bottom was a letter addressed to Scrooge, in Fred's hand.

With jittery fingers, he unfolded the parchment.

'*Dear Uncle Ebenezer,*

If you are reading this, then my time in this world has ended.

Do not grieve for me, dear Uncle, for I have known great joy and love in my life, much of which I owe to you. Your transformation has been a blessing to us all, and your kindness has touched countless lives. But I fear you have not yet forgiven yourself for the man you once were. Let me tell you this: your past does not define you, nor does it diminish the good you have done. Live on, Uncle, not in sorrow, but in the light of the love we have shared.

Carry forward the spirit of Christmas, not just for me, but for all those needing hope.

You will find amongst my belongings a small, hand-carved ornament of the Babe in Bethlehem, a reminder that Christ made it possible for each of us to be redeemed, even a man as hardened and bitter as you once were. May it cast its fondness upon your tree in the darkest of Yuletide seasons, a reminder of the enduring power of love and the promise of eternal life.

With all my love, always,
Your Fred.'

Tears were streaming copiously down Scrooge's face as he finished reading.

Fred's words, though immensely painful, had ignited something more.

The spirit of Christmas, Fred had written, was not a mere season but rather, a calling, a mission to bring light where it was required. A solemn summons to follow in the footsteps of the Savior of the World.

Scrooge's grief, though still ashamedly deep, could not be a roadblock.

It was to become a veritable catalyst.

***

Several mornings later, Scrooge ventured out, the clamor of carriages and the chattering of pedestrians assailing his senses again. This place could be brutal and invasive.

Yet inside him, his heart was singing. He had a purpose.

Though the city's noise and haste usually seemed unbearable in his fragile state, he was happy to engage with the world today, stepping beyond the confines of his old solitary existence.

With each footfall on the icy and snow-covered pavements, a burden had lifted, allowing the chill of the morning air to invigorate his spirit.

Amidst the throng and tumult, he thought of his old partner Marley and the chains he had borne, those heavy links of greed and regret. He shivered at nearly following in his ghostly footsteps.

With an upbeat stride, he made his way to Lily's modest dwelling, familial laughter again wafting through the door as it always did.

There, he found her tending to Fred's children, those bright-eyed cherubs embodying untainted joy.

As Scrooge stepped into the parlor, he was immediately enveloped in the heartbeat of family life.

The moment he crossed the threshold, Lily's children, sensing gaiety in their benefactor's demeanor, erupted into enthusiastic cheers, their little voices rising in a delightful cacophony, its melody long forgotten. "Uncle Scrooge! Uncle Scrooge! Have you brought gifts?"

Their bright eyes sparkled with innocence and naughty mischief, as if they held within them the secret of a coming delight, barely contained.

They came rushing toward him, tiny hands pulling at his coat, skinny little arms wrapping around his legs as though attempting to wrestle him to the ground to see what he had brought for them.

Each cherub vied for his attention, their faces alight with unspoiled affection.

"Look at our shiny marbles! Will you come play with us?" they implored, their hearts unburdened by the worries of the world. "Uncle Scrooge, see, I have a lead carriage to play with!"

He knelt down, knees cracking, his heart swelling with a tenderness assumed long buried.

Happily, he engaged with their bubbling chatter and hand-painted trinkets.

In their innocent jubilation, Scrooge was discovering a world brimming with promise.

The evening flowed like a warm embrace, each moment weaving together the laughter and stories filling Lily's home with a radiant glow. Time, in its relentless march, slipped away unnoticed.

They played games, shared tales, and savored the simple pleasures of togetherness.

Scrooge especially reveled in the joy of the children's imaginations, his heart lightening with each giggle and delighted squeal. Lily, too, joined in the merriment, her laughter a melodic counterpoint to the children's boisterousness, creating a symphony of familial joy stretching into eternity.

Yet, as the quivering candlelight threw peculiar shapes on the walls, reality crept in.

It was time to go home. These days, he did not linger so long at Lily's house since he feared it would make her see him as another mouth to feed; so, he felt the clock's hands creeping closer to the hour of departure, preparing himself for the unpleasant late-night walk.

It was never pleasant striding the streets of old London in the pitch blackness.

Rogues and pickpockets were everywhere, as were cutthroats and conmen, and even if he nipped through the back streets with all the nimbleness of a greyhound, the filth of the streets—things he could not spot in the dark— assailed his fine leather shoes. He tried not to think of it.

He gathered his coat and bid his goodbyes, looking around at the smiling faces, the radiant Lily and her cherubic throng. He was grateful for all of this, for each smile and each breath, for every mouthful of food, every solitary cry of "Uncle!"

It was such a sweet delight to find that at last, he belonged somewhere.

He could only hope this was just the beginning of many more cherished moments to come.

Invigorated by all this sheer goodness, he returned to his home crackling with energy.

Later, in the dim solitude of his bedchamber, the remnants of his former self tangling with the leaping flames and later, with the hearth's dying embers, Scrooge suddenly bolted upright, ablaze with rekindled fervor. The moonlight was streaming in through the window, reaching the utmost corners of the room, casting away every small but dismal vestige of oppressive gloom. Now, even his own place was a home, no longer a pit of despair or a lonely jail, a trap for the elderly and isolated.

There, among the cracked walls bearing witness to countless hours of solitary existence, he raised his hand as if to sweep aside the veil of isolation cloaking him for so long.

"Let this be the dawning of a new season!" he proclaimed with a voice resonating like the ringing of chimes, sounding out clear against the silence of his chamber. "One in which we become the stewards of kindness! For what is wealth if it stands idle while hearts suffer in silence?"

His words, vibrant and alive, broke forth anew from the shackles of years past, years spent hoarding coins like a miser with his hoard. A long-dormant seed had suddenly begun to sprout, reaching toward the dawn of a benevolent day.

There was only one burning question now, one to which he required an answer.

How could he ensure that Fred's legacy—and his own—would endure? How could he lead others to honor Christmas as he and Fred did, and try to retain it all the year?

**

That night, as Scrooge lay in bed, he was visited by a dream. These nightly imaginings had been the scourge of his former life, the one burdened by negativity and gloom.

Now, he lived in fear of their resurgence in case they should awaken the demons in him, the unpleasant and cynical spirit of old. But still, what could a man do but suffer them?

There was no medicine, no concoction to promise a restful, undisturbed sleep.

In this dream, he found himself standing in a vast, shadowy expanse, surrounded by countless minuscule lights; they each seemed to twinkle, blinking on and off in a manner akin to the stars, as if controlled by some vast cosmic device. Each light, he realized, represented a life, some burning brightly, others dim and fragile, or even uncertain, too timid to fully show themselves.

Among them, he witnessed Fred's own light, steady and all-encompassing, guiding him forward.

A patient voice spoke to him from the darkness. "The light of one life can illuminate the path for many. You must carry it forward, Ebenezer. Do not let the light diminish and fade."

When Scrooge awoke, the dream was still lingering.

What was he to make of it?

This time, there was no fear, no cold veins, no palpitations. Just an awareness that somehow, in the depths of the nighttime, he had encountered the eternal spirit of a man, his beloved nephew.

Or at least, that's what he chose to take from his dream.

The road ahead was uncertain, but Scrooge could walk with courage now, allowing the tiny infinite light to be his guide and his savior when times were difficult.

***

In due course and in the manner of all things, autumn seemed to glide past with an air of ethereal grace, akin to a stately ship navigating the vast, shadowy expanse of the ocean under the cloak of night. The leaves, hushing whispers of farewell, skipped in the crisp breeze, swirling and twirling as if caught in a gentle waltz. As the sun dipped below the horizon, its fiery glow surrendered again to night's silken embrace, assuming its indigo canvas.

Here, upon the unpainted backdrop of dark blue turning to black, the stars would soon take their rightful places, once more like distant fireflies heralding the way for dreamers.

In such a wondrous manner did this season pass quietly yet resplendently, unbeknownst to many, bearing the weight of both beauty and fleeting moments. It was as if every sigh of wind carried with it the secrets of the world, inviting all to pause and reflect amid these swift currents of existence.

As the final ember of autumn blinked out and winter's chill began weaving its glassy tendrils through the fabric of the air, Scrooge found himself engaging in deep conversations about his recent dream. He had found the inner strength to talk about it with close confidants, including Bob Cratchit and Lily. They listened intently, their eyes alight, immersed and enraptured.

With their encouragement and understanding, he marinated in the dream's significance, allowing it to settle upon him like the first delicate snowflakes of the season.

Something incredible was happening; no longer was he afraid of the night. If the dreams were to come now, they would be graceful and full of beauty, imbued with minuscule stars of varied tones.

Each morning tugged along with it the reluctance of night's passing, yet within him kindled a flicker of quiet defiance against the encroaching cold. Not just against the encroaching wintry weather, but also against everything hostile and depressing in nature.

He pondered the meaning of that spectral voice, tracing the contours of its message in the quiet solitude of his heart. Christmas, once a mere inconvenience, could now approach in glee!

With each passing day, witnessing the glow of shop windows adorned with lights, and hearing the joyous sounds of caroling, his resolve was solidifying, no longer carrying pain and regrets.

He would never permit Fred's love to die within London; instead, he would render it eternal.

Chapter 4: A Visit Most Mysterious

The air was especially bitter on that Christmas Eve afternoon, a sharp frost that had rarely been felt before. Scrooge barely sensed the cold these days because inside of him, an inferno was at work, protecting his spirits and warming sinews and veins.

And although the city was bustling with last-minute revelers and merchants hawking their wares, Scrooge's home presented an oasis of stillness amidst the cacophony.

His life had turned around for the better, and for this, he could be eternally glad.

Or so he thought.

So, why was it, then, that in the late afternoon after his return, he dozed off in bliss by the fire, only to awake shortly afterwards feeling the all-too-familiar and afeared sensation of dread?

It pervaded his body and mind in equal measure, working its way through every limb until he was shaking. Perhaps he had hoped for too much, too soon. Perhaps he had been complacent. Had he?

The old enemy, dread, had found its way back in, slithering into his core like a malevolent snake. He was mulling on things again, letting bad thoughts enter, allowing them to fester.

Until now, he had been considering his endeavors a success.

Have I been deceiving myself? he wondered. *Surely, if I have made even a small difference in bringing cheer and hope to Christmastime, I would not be shaking like a man possessed!*

He felt forced to admit that his efforts in unraveling the tangled web of cupidity ensnaring the bustling heart of London had, to this disconcerting point, yielded naught but fruitless musings.

Guilty, his mind said to him. *Guilty of self-congratulatory behavior before even making one shred of difference to anything! How could you even think it feasible to so quickly change man's predilections, to steer them off the path of gluttony and avarice, toward something pure and generous?*

Fool that you are, Ebenezer Scrooge. A poor, deluded fool.

You have conned yourself.

Would he, a solitary seeker in this vast scene woven with threads of ambition and desire, ever stumble upon the elusive remedy sought and revered by so many yet grasped by so few?

The heavy burden of worry settled on his face, brewing up a tempest of anxiety.

Beads of sweat were forming on his lined brow, anxious eyes darting, unable to settle.

So then, here I am, a self-proclaimed idiot, doomed to forever remain a spectator in life's game.

Before I took it upon myself to change, at least I knew who I was.

Now, I am but a hopeless wisp, drifting this way and that, seeking a safe place to settle.

He continued walking the filthy streets, stopping now and then to peer into shop windows, hoping to feel that inner glow of satisfaction that he had known for the shortest time. It eluded him. In its place was a frigidity that traveled through his bones as if he were deeply afraid of something.

I have lost myself amid a throng of fervent souls, and must resign myself to the notion that the right solution is destined to slip through my fingers like sand through an hourglass, forever out of reach.

And while I wallow in self-pity, the acquisitiveness of this place continues burgeoning unchecked.

***

Having spent the early hours of the evening in the company of Lily and her brood, Scrooge was sitting alone in his chair next to the fire, gazing into the flames. They crackled and spat in contrast to the chill settling in his chest. A mug of mulled wine, long since forgotten, was resting on the table beside him, its spices no longer fragrant. It was acrid now, smelling far too pungent, having turned to vile vinegar.

Scrooge had attempted to busy himself with his ledger; seeking solace in numbers was a habit to which he was accustomed, and sometimes, it had worked to take his mind off unpleasant things.

Alas, the distraction was ineffectual against the tidal wave of unrest surging in him.

Vivid thoughts, doom-laden, of a world burdened by the greed of industry elites flashed through his mind—thoughts of people hoarding wealth for themselves while joyful spirits lay dormant, hidden beneath layers of gluttony, indifference and hideous self-interest.

As the clock on the mantel struck eleven, each chime jolted the room with a peculiar gravity, like a solemn reminder of the urgent need to combat his ever-spreading malaise. Society had allowed itself to stray so far. Society had lost its way, gorging on whatever it could acquire.

"It is lost then, a lost cause," he said aloud to himself. "This is why it never works for me, for every man acts only out of his own self-satisfaction, and it takes a whole society to effect such change. Aye, a lost cause if we cling to this canker at the heart of our commercial spirit, this insidious poison of the age! This blind worship of Mammon gnaws at our shared humanity, leaving only a barren wilderness. A blight upon the land, demanding a revolution not of blood, but of the very heart!"

He wanted to keep trying, wanted to keep hoping. But it all felt pointless.

Suddenly, the candlelight flickered, though no draft disturbed the room.

Scrooge straightened instantaneously, immediately alert, immediately … aware.

His keen senses, sharpened by years of solitude and vigilance, saw that the shadows in the room had deepened, and an unearthly stillness had descended.

It was a hush so profound that even the crackling fire had been oddly subdued.

Then, from the corner of his vision, he caught sight of a figure in the shadows.

Cloaked and hooded, the stranger's form seemed at the same time both solid and spectral, as though existing both in his world and beyond, walking the line between two various planes of existence.

It glided across the parlor's span with what seemed to be a deliberate grace, its footfalls silent on the bare floorboards as if able to command the air to fall into a reverent hush.

The fabric of the long coarse cloak rippled and undulated, a shadowy veil appearing to drink in the light, surrounding the figure in an aura of enigmatic, mysterious power.

Scrooge, though his heart was leaping within, strangely found himself neither afraid nor startled. Instead, he was transfixed by the apparition, as though his spirit recognized its presence before him.

"Ebenezer Scrooge," the figure intoned, its voice a resonant timbre that seemed to carry both wisdom and solemnity. Had it been a living man, Scrooge would have considered him wise.

"Ebenezer Scrooge," it repeated. "I have come."

Scrooge rose, his hand clutching the back of his chair for support. "So I see." Was he afraid? Perhaps a little. "Who are you?" he demanded, keeping his voice steady despite the moment's peculiarity.

"What business do you have here, and why on this night of all nights?"

With a fluid motion showing grace unmatched, the figure raised a gloved hand, its fingers long and elegant as though sculpted by some unseen artisan, delighting in crafting the ethereal.

In a single, sweeping gesture, it drew back its hood, unveiling a visage defying both the freshness of youthful exuberance and the liver-spotted weariness of age.

But how can this even be possible? Scrooge asked himself. *He is neither old nor young ... neither man nor boy! This ... creature ... defies all logic!*

The visitor was male-like but exuding a captivating amalgamation of all humanity's traits, a rare blend transcending the limitations of time and knowledge.

He peered at it as though his eyes could not be torn away, perhaps transfixed by the rigors of a spell.

The contours of its face bore haunting familiarity, while simultaneously evoking a sense of the unfamiliar, an interplay most intriguing while also unfathomable.

As he gazed upon the countenance, the features shifted subtly, reflecting a thousand faces at once. Each visage was a poignant reminder of lives lived, joys shared, and sorrows borne, each one whispering tales of triumph and despair, laughter and grief, ambition and failure, thereby weaving together the entire collective human experience. Yet, for all this multitude of visages dancing before Scrooge's weary eyes, not a single countenance could he definitively identify.

Each one was unique, bearing its own distinct tale, yet the eyes—the eyes!—were always deep and penetrating, quietly speaking of some profound knowledge and sadness.

Within those sorrowful orbs flickered dimensions of hope, kindling a latent compassion long ago buried, now grown calloused with the weight of his own heartache.

Did this spectral figure stand as a solemn witness to the innumerable hearts cast aside in the relentless pursuit of profit and ambition? Was it a living fresco, painted from the ephemeral struggles of the many made to toil in anguish beneath greed's harsh glare?

A shiver crept up his spine, a cold draught, wrapping about him.

The myriad unseen stories of pain and longing soon lay heavy around his shoulders as if they were ten river-soaked woolen blankets, equally burdensome, equally cold, equally inhospitable and incapable of improving his condition in any way.

Somehow, the mere fact of the being's presence roused an urgent spark in him, beseeching him to rise and do good. Yet it made no sense since the figure merely stood, doing and saying nothing.

Cloaked in an aura of ethereal luminescence, it had now fixed its gaze upon him with an intensity that seemed to pierce the thick fog of his recent despondency.

Its eyes continued tunneling into his soul, urging him with a silent command toward a path of redemption. Now, it was showing an inviting road.

Still, it said not a word more, but he heard in his mind, *come, take it. Follow the path!*

No sooner had he taken up what seemed to be the unspoken message, than the specter began to speak. "Behold me, Scrooge!" it whispered, its voice woven from threads of the past, present, and future all in one. "The world has need of your heart; your spirit can light the way through despair's dim recesses. Do not let the shadows of mankind's making blind you to the radiance that can be; rise up now, rise to receive again the kindness you have embraced in the many years since your last ethereal awakening. For in that embrace lies the power to heal what has been rent asunder, most viciously decimated and destroyed by the anguish formerly holding you captive."

A tremor passed through Scrooge. He was standing on the precipice of transformation, caught in that liminal space between the man he was and the one he could yet become.

"I am The Wanderer," the voice asserted like thunder, bizarrely unsettling, a gravitas commanding attention. "I am a spirit of the future, a keeper of possibilities. Dwelling in a far-off place beyond the confines of time, I exist in a realm untethered by the days' linear progression, in the twilight of space in which past, present, and future converge and intertwine like gossamer threads of fate.

"Here, the myriad strands of choice and consequence are woven into an intricate vision of all existence, shining with potential yet concealed by the shadow of what may yet come to pass."

As it spoke, an unseen force seemed to shift the air, thickening it with an almost electric anticipation. The Wanderer gestured expansively, as if casting light on a great panorama of possibilities, revealing fleeting images before Scrooge's eyes.

It offered glimpses of lives unfolding in a kaleidoscope of choices, moments outwardly branching akin to the great arms of an ancient tree, limbs laden and bowing with the fruits of consequence.

"Consider this well, dear Scrooge," it continued, aiming to find a settling place in the recesses of his heart. "Every decision, every moment of kind act or cruelty, sends ripples outward, across the fabric of time. When the human race chooses to act with kindness, the light spreads wide and bright, like the dawning sun upon a weary land, fostering connections, nurturing hope, and encouraging joy to take root. Conversely, when humankind turns its back on those in dire need, darkness seeps into the crevices of existence, stifling joy, wreaking torment on the wretched."

Powerful visions began to coalesce in Scrooge's mind, flashing scenes of both triumph and despair: families joyously gathered around a humble table, laughter spilling out into the world like music, creating a symphony of togetherness; a weary traveler returning home to a chorus of welcomes, embraced by love and gratitude after an arduous journey.

Yet, as swiftly as the melody soared, it was overtaken by stark shadows of isolation and regret. He beheld the sobering sight of a young mother trapped in a squalid attic, her children curled up around her, hunger gnawing at their bellies as they listened to distant celebratory strains from the streets below.

Nearby, an elderly gentleman sat alone in a dim chamber, surrounded by the suffocating silence of his opulence, riches amassed through callous disregard for the plight of those less fortunate.

The lavish feasts enjoyed by the elite, Scrooge recognized, draped cruel veils across the lives of the forsaken, a constant reminder of how the scales of fortune disparately tipped.

This left countless souls languishing in the margins of society, swallowed whole by the anguish of unfulfilled dreams, ambitions and wishes long since abandoned, a community fractured by the chilling grip of materialism's neglect. The Wanderer's eyes, profound and penetrating, bore into the depths of Scrooge's soul as if probing for the humanity lying dormant therein.

"You must comprehend, Scrooge," it urged, "that the future is not a single path meandering forward but rather an infinite multitude of roads branching in every conceivable direction. Each choice leads inexorably to another, and another, each act of kindness or cruelty shaping all the lives intertwining with yours. Imagine, if you will, a chess game played on an infinite board, where all decisions, all subtle shifts in intention, alter the outcome not just for you but also for each generation yet to arrive."

The Wanderer paused, allowing its message an opportunity to sink in.

"Though I am but a spirit dwelling in the realm of futures unmade, I come to you now as a guide, imploring you to reflect on the path you have chosen to tread thus far.

"The legacy you leave is not merely the gradual accumulation of wealth or possessions, but rather is made up of the benevolence and kindness you cultivate in others' hearts. The spirit of Christmas—that of unbridled generosity, love, and community—can become a radiance banishing the bleakness of avarice and despair. But this calls for your hand, your will to weave it back into society, to challenge the cold ambition of those seeking to starve compassion of its rightful place."

With that, The Wanderer extended a hand, an invitation beckoning Scrooge to step boldly into the vibrant possibilities sprawled before him.

"Altering humankind's destiny, dear Scrooge, is within your grasp," it implored, the earnest fervor of its voice piercing through the fog enshrouding his core. "Teach mankind to embrace the spirit of Christmas, not merely as a season to be observed, but also as a guiding principle upon which everyday decisions shall rest. For so long as there is breath within your body, the future remains an uncharted canvas, a blank slate awaiting the deliberate and loving brushstrokes of your choices."

Scrooge, who for upwards of ten years had swept away all lingering shadows of the spectral world from his thoughts, convinced they were banished with his former self, now found himself nodding slowly. He had learned through his own redemption that there was much in heaven and earth beyond the grasp of mortal understanding.

"What precisely are you asking of me?" he asked cautiously.

"I have come with an offer and a warning," The Wanderer intoned, stepping closer.

Its presence encased the room in a curious blend of serenity and immediacy, pulsing with many unspoken truths. "You stand at a precipice, Ebenezer, acutely aware of the fragile nature of your legacy.

"Your prior transformation, though highly commendable, is merely the start of a far more profound odyssey on which you must embark. You have indeed touched the lives of many, yet you cling to the notion that the legacy you so fervently strive to forge is set in stone like some cosmic decree. Take heed, for it is not yet within time's weft; its permanence is as tenuous as the morning haze, and must be cultivated with intention and care, lest it dissolve in the ether of forgotten moments."

Scrooge's brow furrowed.

"Not enduring?" he echoed, incredulous. "I have given of my fortune and my beating heart. I have lifted the downtrodden and inspired the prosperous to charity. What more can any man do?"

The Wanderer regarded him with an inscrutable expression.

"Acts of kindness, however great, are fleeting if those who follow do not carry forth the flame. A chain of compassion must bind together the departed, the living, and all those as yet unborn. This sacred link, forged from the purest of intentions, needs to pass through generations until the end of time. Your beloved London grows restless, its people swayed by forces of the dark. Even now, your name, once revered, is being spoken with doubt among those who profit from indifference."

Scrooge sank back into his chair, the firelight casting deep shadows across his face.

"Then what must I do? Tell me! For I cannot bear the thought of failing those who look to me. For weeks past, this vexing dilemma has gnawed at my soul, a serpent of doubt strangling my internal organs, coiling tighter. I have sought an answer, a solution to endure through the ages, a balm to soothe this torment gnawing relentlessly at my peace."

The Wanderer gestured, the room beginning at first to shimmer, then to dissolve.

Scrooge's modest bedchamber became replaced by a swirling expanse of light and shadow, visions of the future flitting by like scenes glimpsed through a tiny, frosted window.

Factories were towering ever higher, their smoke choking the sky.

He saw streets teeming with the destitute, their eyes hollow and desperate.

Among these images, he caught sight of a woman he recognized as Lily, the embodiment of loss, her previous vibrancy now dulled by poverty's relentless march.

She stood amidst the remnants of her life, meager possessions stripped away by the hands of those who clutched at wealth with iron-fisted resolve, oblivious to the struggles of those beneath.

Scrooge's heart ached, forced to witness her forlorn, heartbroken efforts to maintain dignity in the face of overwhelming despair. The mere shadow of a smile would flicker on her lips as she watched the children of the street, clad in tattered clothes inadequate for the weather, playing with scraps they had scavenged. She was both nourished and wounded by their innocent joy, their ability to create pastimes of marvel and wonder from the most basic and largely destroyed items.

Yet with each beam of laughter that reached her ears, there came a pang of remembrance for she had once held such joy before the heavy yoke of misfortune had lately fastened itself to her.

A cruel wave of regret washed over Scrooge. He could not help but think how different her fate might have been had he intervened long ago, securing for the girl a brighter future.

Alas, there she stood, a widow of both love and circumstance, cast aside again.

It was as if her earthly worth had been unraveled and discarded like remnants of a wedding gown left to rot. It struck him with bitter clarity—the chilling truth that a heart once cherished could so easily be relegated to the shadows in this way. It had not served any purpose, then, that he had revisited her, not if he had since cast her aside a second time, too enmeshed in his own self and countless deeds.

"The tides of wealth and poverty crash against the shore of indifference," The Wanderer stated gravely, breaking into Scrooge's troubled thoughts. "For each soul like Lily, there are countless more who suffer in silence—mothers clutching their children to their breasts in dark alleys, the hungry huddled beneath bridges, the elderly forgotten, lying in their own waste. Each day, they rise to face the stark realities they did not choose for themselves, while the rich bask in the glow of their ill-gotten gains, the warmth of shared conscience an alien notion far beyond their gilded realm."

As Scrooge bore witness to the panorama of neglect, the images shifted, now revealing an alley where the wretched gathered as shadows of human beings, their bodies thin and beaten.

By now, the unflinching gaze of societal indifference had stripped them of even the faintest hope; forsaken under the weight of acquisitiveness, their existence teetered on a precipice of despair.

"You must see, Scrooge," the spirit continued, its voice rising over the mournful display, "that a society allowing such suffering is one bound to feed upon itself. Being consumed by the desire for gain can only foster division, never unity. The health of a people is measured not in the treasures hoarded by a few but in the gentleness and understanding afforded to the most vulnerable among them.

"Therein lies the essence of your Christmastide, an embracing magnanimity that can thaw the cold hearts of the affluent and, in turn, inspire them to lend a helping hand to those struggling against a plight not of their making. Self-sufficiency, a noble virtue to instill and cherish as the highest aspiration of man, must ever coexist with the benevolence of charity, which, when the hand of misfortune descends, shall rise with generous grace to provide solace and succor in each person's hour of need."

The specter's words pierced Scrooge to his marrow, and he faltered.

So, the image of Lily was plaguing him still. Her haunted soul, a caged bird yearning for release, silently pleaded for the balm he now understood he could bestow, the elixir of kindness capable of soothing its wounded spirit and setting it free. A tear developed on his cheek as he wished to be swept away from this awful scene he was witnessing. Hesitation was no longer an option.

Nothing made sense.

The legacy he envisioned was one of boundless kindness extended, a veritable lighthouse of hope for every neglected soul adrift in a tide of indifference. It paved the way toward a more just and tender society, all manner of destitution meeting with open hearts.

In such a world, even a widow like dear Lily would find herself coddled in the embrace of fellowship, once-silent sorrows transformed into belonging.

In that moment of visceral understanding, Scrooge turned to The Wanderer.

"Then let me rise to this challenge!" he exclaimed. "I can do this! Please, show me where I may intercede for those who suffer, where I may reignite the light of compassion in the darkness that breeds despair. If it is—as you say—possible to alter this reality, tell me how I can serve!"

The Wanderer extended a hand, its touch ethereal yet grounding, sending a surge of comfort out as if the light of a thousand suns had just converged upon his spirit.

As the monumental revelation surged through Ebenezer Scrooge to claim every breath of his lungs and every beat of his arterial system, a profound stillness enveloped the chamber.

It was heavy with portentous expectation.

The figure of The Wanderer, bearing an ethereal luminescence that shimmered like dawn's first light, regarded Scrooge with an expression of both sorrow and serenity.

This figure was a collection of opposites, a confusing maelstrom of contradictions.

And finally, Scrooge knew one thing, that there was no point in asking why or how, or what any of this truly meant. The figure's words defied all rational comprehension.

God knew, he had tried …

Without uttering a word, the being began to dissolve, its already radiant glow at first intensifying, spiraling with an entrancing, delicate motion. Gossamer threads of smoke, tendrils of brilliance began weaving an iridescent picture, setting it dancing in a balletic display of splendor.

The atmosphere seemed to shiver with anticipation as the light formed a magnificent whirlwind, beckoning with formidable yet divine allure.

"Oh, wretched man, you must improve! I shall not allow Lily, with her gentle spirit and weary eyes, to become yet another downbeat figure, cast aside like a forgotten waif upon the unforgiving streets. Rather, I am resolute in my determination for you to weave for her and her innocent progeny a future resplendent with opportunity, a scene of hope in which despair shall have no dominion."

Scrooge stood unmoving, transfixed by the cosmic spectacle.

The blinding luminescence encased The Wanderer, eventually drawing him upward, as if the fabric of the universe had conspired to embrace his spirit, coalescing to elevate him into realms unknown.

In a final, stunning flourish, the light culminated in a glorious explosion of brilliance, a breathtaking panorama that left Scrooge momentarily blinded, even the cavernous room becoming devoured whole.

Then, as quickly as it had onset, the phenomenon waned, leaving his chamber softly shrouded once more in familiar calm. Alone now, encompassed by the stillness of the night, Scrooge was beset by inner reflections on the profound occurrence. A quiet rolling of enlightenment clamored in him.

As the quietude pressed upon him, an awakening of purpose surged again, igniting a fire briefly extinguished. No longer could he remain a prisoner of the wealthy's making, a hapless victim ensnared in the web of avidity spun by hoarders of fortunes while neglecting the plight of fellow men.

No longer would he let himself be shackled by the same clutches of greed that had dulled humanity's sensibilities, withering their hearts.

The luminosity of the Wanderer's light lingered, an earnest whisper urging him to embrace the elevation of his spirit, becoming a torch to light the way for the many less fortunate.

Soon, Scrooge reclined upon the cool, worn sheets of his bed, the room transformed in the wake of celestial visitation. The spectral chill of regret still sent a cold breeze across his skin, but it was newly tempered by a fierce glow, defiant in the face of despair casting such a pall over his life of late.

"Tomorrow," he murmured firmly to himself, breathing words bringing the promise of change. "Tomorrow, I shall live anew. I shall reach out to those in want, and in doing so, shall discover true riches surpassing all the gold and silver once coveted."

Scrooge's metamorphosis would shortly bloom with the dawn of a new day, suffused with a spirit so fervently alive.

Chapter 5: A Vision of the Future

By the dim light of a solitary candle, shadows jostling playfully across the walls of his humble bedchamber, Ebenezer Scrooge felt weariness pulling on his eyelids. Yet still, he was lying awake.

Sleep, that increasingly elusive and indifferent companion, had once more slipped through his grasp, refusing to grant him the respite he so desperately craved.

His mind, clouded with the detritus of regrets and the restless whispers of the night, began drifting into a realm more nebulous than that of waking thought. It was a delirium.

Three more hours passed, listening to the hooting of owls and the shrieking of badgers tussling in the grounds. Mercifully, toward last light, he finally surrendered to the gentle arms of slumber.

Yet, even as he acquiesced to that velvety embrace, a faint echo of his pocket watch tolling the somber hour of midnight intruded on his consciousness, a spectral reminder of time's relentless march.

In an instant, a stirring presence took form.

A figure emerged from the ether, imbued with an incredible glow that seemed to pulse with the rhythm of the stars. The Wanderer, that other-worldly apparition of ethereal grace, was back.

Scrooge rubbed his eyes, then sat up in bed, pushing his back against the cold stone wall.

What affront was this? Could a man get no peace, not even in his own bedchamber?

This was preposterous!

"Not you again! I have barely rested" he growled fiercely, clutching at his aching temples, his eyes blazing with a restless fury, as if the very exhaustion had ignited a storm within him.

He gazed upon the enigmatic visitor, irked, yet also gripped by an overwhelming sense of uncertainty. Was this 'thing' but a dream conjured by the remnants of a troubled, over-tired mind?

Or was it perhaps a vision, a portentous harbinger intending to steer his path anew?

Or was it a true ghost come to torment him, to show that wherever he went, it could come too?

That thought aggrieved him. The air was thick with his contemplation, straddling the threshold between reality and fantasy as he beheld the figure's returned celestial illumination.

It was clear now: The Wanderer would not let him go.

It was planning to drag him away, willing or otherwise, to the corners of this fractured world.

Or perhaps beyond. He would glimpse the consequences of his transformation—or the dire lack thereof—as The Wanderer beckoned him into realms of both dread and promise, tugging him in two directions, seeing in which one he would pull. He knew he would be a reluctant traveler, not wishing to see the light of Christmas fighting the encroaching darkness.

He was on the precipice of a journey, the air pregnant with that same electric anticipation, fate's invisible threads pulled taut. In that ephemeral moment, the surroundings began to dissolve, fading into swirling colors and blinding lights that enveloped them both.

Reality itself was swaying.

It was a boat on a quiet tide, begging him to surrender completely to the experience ahead.

And so, as if summoned by an unseen hand, the current of light surged forth, cradling Scrooge and The Wanderer in its luminous hold and propelling them into a vast, uncharted expanse—a world neither betwixt nor between, neither here nor there, a state of being hovering in languid indecision.

Here, time's boundaries unraveled as though from a spool. Scrooge felt a peculiar weightlessness, as though his mortal form had been left behind, yet his senses were sharper than ever.

Every fiber of his being seemed attuned to the strangest coursing energies.

"For where are we bound?" he asked, shocked by how his voice ricocheted in the ethereal void, quaking with the tremor of uncertainty accompanying his travels to the threshold of knowledge.

"To a place where futures unfold," The Wanderer replied as if the answer were obvious and carried meaning, its tone heavy with both promise and forewarning.

"Prepare yourself, Ebenezer, for what you are about to witness may simultaneously enlighten and burden you. Some mere mortals are not fated to cast their eyes upon the myriad possibilities hinging upon the whims of both present and future. For to behold such a panoply of outcomes is a privilege reserved for those rare souls whose spirits keep pace with the cadence of time and consequence."

The swirling lights coalesced into a scene of startling clarity.

Scrooge was standing in a familiar street, one he had walked countless times, but it was a street transformed.

Underfoot, it was cracked and uneven, the buildings darkened by soot and neglect.

Children, faces gaunt and eyes listless, huddled in doorways, afflicted by the sores of malnutrition. Women with hollow cheeks and frayed shawls bartered for scraps in a market devoid of cheer.

"This is London, the true London," Scrooge whispered, his voice catching in his throat.

The Wanderer nodded. "This is a future where your transformation never took place. Where the miser Ebenezer Scrooge once perpetuated his life of avarice."

As Scrooge's heart twisted with remorse, he saw a familiar figure among the destitute, a stooped woman with sorrow etched deeply into her features.

She clutched two ragged children to her breast, their faces pale and wan.

It was Fred's widow, Lily. Again.

"No," Scrooge murmured, stepping closer and subconsciously reaching out to comfort her, though his presence went unnoticed by the scene before him. "Not Lily. Not Fred's family."

"Without your support," The Wanderer explained, "Fred's death left Lily and the children destitute. The charity you would have provided was never offered. They fell victim to poverty's relentless grind."

Scrooge turned to the spirit, anguish etched on his face.

"Yes, I know! You have displayed this to me once already," Scrooge lamented, an edge of desperation in his tone. "Is this repetition to drive the point home with a greater fervor? For I assure you, I am unable to endure the weight of it all once more. A man has limits, and I have reached mine.

"Surely, someone else could have helped them! Surely, others could have taken up the mantle! Could it be that in this vast and teeming metropolis, there exists not a one other soul with a spark of compassion, not one who would cast a kindly eye upon a widow in distress?"

A chilling thought, indeed, that in this supposed haven of civilization, such destitution could fester.

"I present this vision of potentiality once more, repetition serving as the wellspring of enlightenment, the progenitor of deeds, and thus the very craftsman of achievement," The Wanderer said, pausing to let those solemn words settle into the heart of his listener.

"Indeed, it is true that compassion often lies dormant, awaiting a flicker of inspiration, a guiding hand to stoke its dwindling embers into a resplendent blaze. For without your metamorphosis, my dear friend, that vital spark remained unlit, languishing in the shadows of indifference; yet, when embraced by the light of one benevolent soul, it has the power to set aglow the hearts of many. In this way, charity and kindness bloom, spreading like a thriving vine, fortifying its roots as it intertwines with the eager hands of those who nurture it until it grows sturdy and grand, enveloping all within its generous embrace and fostering a community resplendent in acts of love and goodwill."

As these words settled heavily upon Scrooge's shoulders, the scene dissolved into a whirlwind of color before reforming into another future.

Here, Scrooge saw a bustling factory, its chimneys spewing black smoke into the already polluted sky. Inside, men, women, and children toiled in conditions so harsh that Scrooge recoiled in horror.

Their faces bore expressions of resignation, bodies bent and broken by unending labor. In fact, while their bodies were here, in this godforsaken place, their minds were elsewhere or had closed off to the barrenness of industry's chore. They went about their work with glazed eyes, leaden feet.

These were the living who had already passed, having nothing for which to exist.

"Is this the bleak future of doom that awaits me if I falter in my purpose?"

Scrooge's voice quavered with dread and despair.

"Am I to be the architect of such sorrow, an unwitting harbinger of desolation stretching infinitely before me, despoiling the hopes and dreams of those whose lives brush up against mine? Pray tell, must I bear witness to this grim tableau and shoulder my failure, knowing that each action I take impresses upon not only my own spirit but also the hearts of the countless intertwined souls?"

The Wandered huffed.

"You already know this is the world shaped by unchecked ambition!" The Wanderer said, exasperated. "Though you have changed, the forces of greed and industry have not, and their reaches are vast. Your transformation alone, though noble, is not sufficient to stem the tide. I also sense that despite your many good deeds, you still consider the pains within your own self in greater proportion than the suffering of those you purport to assist! Have you heard yourself? 'Me, me, me,' you cry!

"Have you not always known all this? What, did you believe you could save the world as if it were a mere trifle? That you could just proclaim, 'world, I am here to bring you hope' without endeavoring to do anything? Without really wanting it, only seeking to make your own self feel and appear better? So, you give up now after so many brave, bold words? You disappoint me."

He stared fixatedly at Scrooge, like a schoolmaster giving a boy a ticking off.

Scrooge looked away, unwilling to hear it. But still, The Wanderer had not finished!

"The delicate balance of the universe, once a harmonious symphony of give and take, now groans under insatiability gluttony. Those blessed with fortune, blinded by an unquenchable lust for wealth and power, have forsaken generosity's path. Instead, they hoard their riches, leaving a trail of despair in their wake. The foundations of society tremble, threatened by this monstrous imbalance, a chilling portent of the chaos awaiting if this plague of greed is not swiftly eradicated."

As the chilling mists of time gathered around them, The Wanderer, shrouded in shadows and whispers, beckoned Scrooge forward into the bleak outlook of a future unspooled from the threads of indifference and cupidity. They stepped beyond the veil of what might be.

With this, they ventured into a dismal landscape.

Before them lay a squalid expanse, where crumbling edifices stood as husks of a once-thriving society, hundreds of dilapidated façades bearing silent witness to neglect's ravages.

The streets, lined with the remnants of discarded, yielded and fruitless dreams, had become devoid of laughter and life. Here, poverty had eroded all, leaving behind hollow visages and sunken eyes.

Each person's face reflected a profound resignation.

"In this forlorn realm, dear Scrooge," murmured The Wanderer hauntingly, "the poor have relinquished all their rights, bartering their dignity in exchange for the fleeting scraps that their betters cast aside when they even deign to feed them. They are but shadows of their former selves, cogs in a great machine, ground down by those who wield power from their ivory towers.

"When the somber hour approaches, grim reality forcing the ultimate choice upon them—between humble sustenance to nourish their beloved kin or the lofty ideals of their God-given rights—they, weighed down by necessity's cruel hand, surrender with reluctance their noble aspirations for a meager morsel of bread; yet, in that fateful decision, they unwittingly embrace the chains of bondage that will forever bind their spirits. Thus, in their own way, we can say the impoverished too are greedy. Faced with gruel and bread or their rights, they too make a choice."

Scrooge was livid, boiling inside.

"You, sir, you cannot in good faith compare the choices of the rich—who over-indulge and pillage and steal, and who run their belching factories where they grind men down along with the grain—with those of the people so bowed and emaciated that they can barely crawl to the workhouse? Of course, they would choose bread! Of course, they would choose gruel! In their shoes, what would you do?"

The Wanderer shrugged before opining, "Sir, you may not have noticed I am not in their shoes. I do not know what they have done or not done to end up in such a pathetic predicament. And the reason for that, my good gentleman, is due to my hard work, the diligence I have applied throughout life, and the same diligence my father applied, and his father before him and—"

Scrooge clapped his hands over his ears. "Stop, I beseech you. Just stop."

In his mind, he was thinking, *diligence, my foot!*

You are but a specter, so since when did you have to do real work? Since when were you born of a hardworking man, and of his equally labor-driven grandfather before him? You lie and cheat!

But even if we opine that it is true, you have been saved from an impoverished state by those who worked before you.

Gold sovereigns passed hand to hand through the family have saved many a dumb man's life.

If this is your past, you may as well have purloined it, wrested it from the hands of a man in hunger.

Your inherited means are far from being your own, 'fine sir' ...

I can barely believe the heinous words you speak.

He turned to The Wanderer with a look of disdain. But all the words he would dearly love to say failed him. What was the sense in crossing words with someone even mildly of these opinions?

But he could not remain incensed for The Wanderer did not seem to be a cruel being, only unaware. These were the accepted opinions of every man not confined to the workhouse or to such poverty. How could they know better? Besides, Scrooge chose to believe he heard compassion and sadness in The Wanderer, that this was indeed why he chose to show Scrooge this lamentable scene.

Dressed in self-interest, most would simply have turned a blind eye.

At least The Wanderer acknowledged their situation, and at least his eyes looked sad about it. And, he might be conducting himself in the very manner best suited to impress upon Scrooge the dire gravity of the situation, and to imbue him with those most essential lessons.

As they wandered deeper into this grim tableau, Scrooge beheld a procession of wretched souls, trudging through muck and mire, their backs stooped under the burden of servitude.

They wore the tattered remnants of once-proud clothing, their hands sore and worn, toiling beneath the watchful gazes of the elites. The employers proudly wore the squalor they offered like an outfit, their cries ringing hollow against the suffering of men, women, and little children.

As Scrooge witnessed this lamentable scene, a wave of icy dread washed over him.

An aged man, bowed beneath a crushing roll of iron and cloth, had collapsed in the street, his spirit seemingly crushed beneath relentless demands. "Behold, this man," The Wanderer said, failing to follow up with anything at all by way of explanation. He also too looked defeated by it.

The man's fellow laborers, their faces grim with fear of reprisal, marched past without a single glance, their own survival paramount. Scrooge, his heart wrenched with a pain long forgotten, reached out a trembling hand to offer succor to the fallen man. But before his intentions could be realized, The Wanderer, with a knowing gaze, diverted his attention elsewhere. And Scrooge was powerless.

Where the Wanderer told him to look, he looked, unable to fight his urge.

It was not a choice he could even make for himself; The Wanderer exerted such control.

"Look closely, Scrooge," The Wanderer urged next, gesturing toward a cluster of gaunt figures huddled together beneath a flickering gaslight. "Such is the fate awaiting a world indifferent to the plight of the downtrodden. These poor souls have been stripped not only of their possessions but equally of their essence, reduced to instruments of profit in the hands of the uncaring."

Scrooge's heart ached to witness their plight, a churning tempest of emotions welling.

He felt a longing to extend a hand, to offer solace, yet was frozen in place by this grim reality.

"It is not merely their wealth that has been stolen," The Wanderer continued, deep sorrow etched into the lines of his visage. "So too has their right to aspire to a life of meaning been eroded. Each day, they awaken to a drudgery so relentless, it extinguishes each small flame of hope before it can take hold. They have lost their light, supplanted by darkness. A once radiant glow, showing the way to not only their own paths but also casting conviviality upon the lives of others, has faded, leaving behind naught but a dim memory of joy. This is the legacy born of ignorance and neglect, a cycle feeding upon itself, devouring the spirit of mankind. Yet just as I said, the poor must make a decision."

With that, The Wanderer gestured again, drawing Scrooge's attention to a grand estate rising in the distance, its opulence starkly contrasting the surrounding melancholy.

This was a gilded cage in which the powers that be reveled in their excess, entirely oblivious—or claiming to be—to the suffering beyond their walls. Through the enormous windows adorned with fine silk drapery, Scrooge caught glimpses of lavish banquets, the wealthy feasting on delicacies that glistened like jewels. Their laughter could be heard ringing out with an unsettling lightness, as if mocking the mournful strains of the lives they had so carelessly cast aside.

With each clink of crystal and every honeyed word, they pointed fingers of scorn at those whose hands, worn and roughened from toil, could only dream of such grandeur.

It was a cruel reminder that wealth could so easily blind them.

Scrooge recognized some of them; these were the industrialists who had resisted his philanthropy, who saw the poor as simple tools to be used and later, when they were broken, to be discarded.

"Do you not see, Scrooge?" he inquired, his voice foreboding. "The avarice enshrining the wealthy elite separates them from their fellow men, yet, in the shadows of their splendor, they are naught but prisoners of their making, encaged by insatiable desires. You see, they also cannot escape their fate. Each coin exchanged fortifies the chains binding others, yet they remain blissfully unaware, their eyes clouded by the lust for more—a more that shall never quench their infinite thirst.

"Scrooge, as I said, the industrialists have their own paths already carved out. They know no better, or, perchance, had so ruthlessly stifled the faint stirrings of conscience within them that the cries of decency and fellow-feeling were utterly drowned, leaving only a bleak, uncaring void where pity once might have resided. I sensed the wrath in you when I, just toying with an answer, said I could never wear their shoes. I wished to see how you responded, and I did see. What I meant was although I see the plight of the poor, if I were or had been an industrialist, a factory owner, I too would be driving my cart in a rut."

Scrooge nodded. Some of what The Wanderer said made sense.

And thus, the affluent, too, found themselves trapped in the gilded cage of custom and convention, blindly pursuing the dictates of their station, rather than charting a course of their own conscious choosing. Was that what he meant?

Overwhelmed by the scene before him, Scrooge felt the frigid grip of dread encircling him. However much he may have understood, this did not lighten the dreadful scourge upon the poor!

"Alas, is it then truly beyond the bounds of human endeavor? Can the suffering multitude never be raised from their abject state, nor the souls of the prosperous purged of their hardened indifference? Nay, I say! Am I not, myself, a living testament to the possibility of turning from a wretched path? Am I not proof of the ability to change one's very course?" he finally implored, desperation clawing at his throat.

"Ah, therein lies the crux of it, dear Scrooge," The Wanderer replied, his gaze piercing through the darkness. "Change begins not in the realm of the wealthy, but in the hearts of the ordinary men and women who possess the power to rise up, to reclaim their rights and forge a new path through the ashes of despair. But first, they must be shown the light, you see! One cannot expect the wealthy to suddenly see through a poor man's eyes, can one? They need to be made to do so!

"Therein lies your choice, dear Scrooge, a hard choice for you too—whether to walk in indifference or to kindle a flame of compassion in these wretched poor souls."

As Scrooge's own prior decisions reverberated through the desolation, he knew—not only for himself but also for the countless souls suffering in hidden places—that the time had come for a reckoning, the kind that could alter the course of destiny.

"Even now," The Wanderer continued, "there are those who oppose you, who see kindness as weakness and charity as folly. They grow stronger, their influence widening with each passing day. Before long, the sands of time shall trickle through the hourglass, and the moment shall arrive when it will irrevocably be too late; at that hour, the fate of all of humanity, once rich with potential, will be sealed within the merciless grip of destiny, leaving no prospects to light the path ahead.

"The downtrodden afflicted must understand, sir, that liberation from this relentless nightmare—a plight most dire, indeed—cannot simply be bestowed upon them by the capricious whims of fate or the inclemency of fortune. No, it must be fervently claimed, wrested from the wealthy's iron grasp.

"And how do you achieve this, Scrooge? Through an uprising, I say! For the chains binding the poor workers are forged not merely of metal but also of being blind sighted to their own innate power, as well as by apathy and resignation. It is only through a collective, their indomitable spirit rising in defiance, that they may shatter those shackles long holding them in thrall. Let them raise their voices as one, igniting the spark of revolution, for it is in the bold assertion of their rights and the courage to challenge their oppressors that the dawn of true freedom may unburden their weary souls."

Scrooge's shoulders sagged under what he had seen and heard.

The Wanderer spoke as if the whole burden, the responsibility for relieving the agony of the poor rested solely on him, Scrooge! How could that be?

He was not the only man in London town who saw the terrible treatment of these people, surely?

His head hung low, his troubles bearing down upon him inexplicably hard—with no mercy—casting him into a state of near defeat. Philanthropy was one thing, but this … this required a miracle of God, no less! Any spark of promise for betterment seemed but a distant ember, struggling against the encroaching tide of gloom, like a child's sandcastle hoping to withstand the incoming sea.

It was ridiculous, impossible, pointless.

But from deep in his mind, a small and plaintive voice asked, *but if every man says he cannot do it, just as I have said, then what? What shall become of these people? What does it mean for all of us?*

He said aloud, as if speaking to the Almighty, "What hope is there? If my efforts alone are insufficient, if the forces arrayed against compassion are so vast, what can this one man do?"

The Wanderer turned to him, its face shifting into quiet determination.

"One man alone cannot save a city, Ebenezer. But one man can inspire others to rise. The light of Christmas is not yours alone to bear—it is a spark to be passed from hand to hand, heart to heart. If you wish to change the future, you must ignite the same in them."

"Let me think about it," Scrooge offered, at least a minuscule part of him hoping this could still free him from the task no one else seemed likely to take on. "I will revert to you with a decision…"

The Wanderer burst out in a derisory laugh.

"Ha! My dear Ebenezer. None of us is promised a tomorrow. Decide, and decide now, for the time to start is … it has passed already. Have you never wondered what is this thing called time? What purpose it serves? Each man seeks to know time intimately, eyeing the finest watches in the jeweler's window. Because one day, his time will have run out. All the sand, one day, will have run dry in each hourglass. And yours, Scrooge, has run out as far as this proposition is concerned. I need an answer."

***

It had been but an hour since his meeting with The Wanderer. Scrooge felt ready.

The Wanderer's rousing speech and his urgent proclamation about time never being enough had stirred something. The visions appearing to Scrooge had shifted once more.

This time, Scrooge beheld a delightful gathering of souls encircled around a modest fire, where laughter mingled harmoniously with the crackling of the flames.

The souls shared humble sustenance and the cherished warmth of camaraderie.

Their faces, though still engraved with a dire weariness, glowed with resilience and a spirit akin to the lights of Christmas, suggesting the dawning of brighter days just beyond the horizon.

It was possible, Scrooge thought. *Everything is possible.*

Why otherwise would this being, The Wanderer, have come specifically to me?

If time is truly so short and the moment upon us, why would he waste time on me if not for ...

He really did not know, but what mattered was that he was reaching a conclusion.

Scrooge's gaze fell upon a vision of Lily, radiant as ever, her arms enveloping a sprightly coalition of children, whose exuberance enchanted the air.

Their eyes sparkled with the brilliance of a thousand stars scattered across a twilight sky, and their laughter danced like gilded leaves in a gentle breeze.

In this jubilant assembly, amidst their shared trials and tribulations, resided a profound unity—a resounding affirmation that tomorrow could bear far sweeter fruit.

"Oh, look!" Scrooge exclaimed, his heart swelling with an unexpected mirth. "What joy abounds in their midst! How the spirit of togetherness lifts them, even in the face of life's tempests! Why, it seems that despite their burdens, their eyes turn toward brighter horizons! Look at them—so steadfast! It's as if their focus, like rays of light piercing through the darkest clouds after a thunderstorm, lightens their spirits! Indeed, amidst their trials, transformation is at hand.

"Their sorrows appear but a distant, faded image, overshadowed by vivacity and camaraderie that wraps around their bodies, a comforting shawl against adversity's chill! Remarkable!"

The scene unfurled, becoming a joyous symphony, bringing the bright buoyancy of optimism.

"You see, are you not gladdened by knowing this is the future you can create?" The Wanderer intoned, a voice imbued with joy and gravity alike. "A future in which the spirit of giving and the joy of community rise like the sun, dispelling isolation and unhappiness? It is a legacy built upon love, woven with the threads of kindness shared among neighbors, friends, and strangers alike."

"Then I must strive to do more!" he said. "I shall seek the means to ensure that compassion burns brightly not just within me, but in all hearts willing to embrace it!"

At this, The Wanderer, with a gesture of profound finality, extended its hand once more, conveying, without a whisper, that its work was finished.

***

In an instant, a fleeting dream dissolving in the dawn's first light, The Wanderer swirled away, enveloped in a cascade of iridescent brilliance that left the air tingling with the residue of magic and epiphany. Before Scrooge could fully comprehend the magnitude of the revelations just encountered, he found himself nestled once more within the familiar confines of his cold and somber bed.

Pallid moonlight lazily spilled through the window, drifting clouds soaring by the white moon. Shadows were forming on the walls, mumbling of remnants of adventures past.

A profound stillness enveloped him, something he had not known before.

There had been too much musing and pondering, too much listening and thinking. Too much stillness and contemplation. Now, he would act.

When the night's long sleep had next cleared from his eyes, that would be the time to begin.

He lay staring at the white ceiling only lit by moonlight, and he was feeling emboldened, renewed, and vigorous for a change. Within the room's stillness thrummed the exhilarating pulse of change.

Here, in the sanctuary of his room, he lay, heart racing with the urgency to begin.

The remnants of visions both wondrous and poignant flitted through his mind, a swell of excitement rising, ready to conquer the world.

Chapter 6: Marley's Return

Before the gentle embrace of much-needed, elusive sleep could descend upon his exhausted body and mind like a soft, silken coverlet created by the heavens, the clock struck one with an almighty gong sounding from the hallway downstairs.

His longcase clock, left to him a decade past by a distant relative, liked to make its noisy presence known; that infernal device would someday be the death of him since whenever sleep eluded him, its chime would drive him to near insanity. Tonight was no different.

Scrooge found himself yet again sleepless in his dimly lit bedchamber, his mind a storm of thoughts, a whirlwind whipped up by anxiety, eagerness, questioning, self-doubt, self-recriminations, and *what-ifs*. By now, he was sitting up, resting his back on the two pillows, glass of water in hand.

The journey with The Wanderer had left him profoundly shaken, yet also deeply resolved, so much so that he now could not settle. He had been so excited but an hour ago, so keen to begin this necessary surge, this uprising! But there was one question neither he nor The Wanderer had explained or even contemplated, so it seemed. The discordant visions of desolation and hope intertwined in his memory, urging him to so much action that he yearned to spring up and commence!

But the unaddressed question was: how? *Alas for guidance! The Wanderer, with all his mysterious knowledge, might well have done no less than impart a fragment of his understanding, sufficient to set my course upon the turbulent waters of reform and change*, he thought, exasperated.

A sudden chill swept through the air, causing his whole body to shiver as the twirling tempests of his uneasy mind wrestled with an inhospitable night, and the promise of so much worse.

The white clouds he had seen earlier through his window now chased swiftly across a barren sky.

The moon had almost hidden herself in fog as if ashamed.

The flames in the hearth leaped high, then faltered, growing feeble and hesitant as if in answer to his disturbing inner turmoil. "Something was amiss, and it has torn me from slumber yet again," he said to his miserable self. "No, something *is* amiss. Something is … here!"

Gradually, a ghostly greenish light began to emanate from the corner of the room.

Scrooge, though seasoned in encounters with the supernatural, felt his pulse quicken—a quickening born not of fear alone but of anticipation as a familiar figure materialized.

The green haze gradually cleared, and in its place stood a transparent Jacob Marley, his face as pale and sorrowful as the night they first had met after Marley's death. The chains that bound him rattled with each spectral step, a mournful symphony that shook the chamber.

"Ebenezer," the ghostly apparition stated, his voice a wail cutting through the stillness, "you linger still in the shadow of your former self, on the cusp of absolute redemption. You have ventured forth with The Wanderer, yet the true journey—nay, the true test for you—lies imminently ahead. Take heed, for the spirits now gather around you, eager to nudge you further along the path that leads to emancipation, for both you and for the multitude of others who look to you."

Those words hanging thickly in the air, Scrooge felt his own existence pressing down upon him. The encumbrance of Marley's chains seemed to harmonize with the shackles binding him throughout his life, shackles forged from self-interest and disregard for his fellow man.

As he met the somber gaze of his deceased partner, a frisson of understanding sparked.

"Jacob, my old friend," Scrooge replied, his voice trembling with the remnants of fear. "What is it that you seek to reveal? How shall I—an old gentleman nearing the end of his days—become this transformational being of whom everyone seems to speak? What must I do to stave off the chilling grip of despair that threatens to claim the human spirit?

"I—I agree it must be done, Jacob, I agree! But no one tells me how!"

Marley's ghost flickered and shimmered, one moment present, another fading as though caught in a relentless battle to manifest on this side of the veil keeping the living from the dead.

His form, at once ethereal and fleeting, wavered in the dim light, striving to coalesce into something more substantial. The bewildered Scrooge watched, his heart pounding with a mix of trepidation and anticipation, as the specter's lips moved in silent requiem; though the words remained trapped within the confines of an otherworldly silence, their unuttered weight dominated, pressing upon Scrooge's soul in a blanket of impending revelation. Here, in this twilight realm, time itself seemed to hold its breath, waiting for the secrets of the afterlife to be laid bare before the ears of the living.

"Jacob!" Scrooge exclaimed, rising from his chair. He was suddenly vexed; all these pieces of sound counsel were turning out to be bland, too unspecific, too … vague, beginning to be irksome.

"Why do you return to me now, after all that has passed? I find myself at a crossroads and must implore you, for I am in desperate need of your direct, clear, specific counsel—your guiding wisdom—if I am to aid in this perilous waltz of existence, the frightfully difficult, onerous task set before me!

"I fear that the those against me far exceed those for me. Therefore, I beseech you, grant me the insight to navigate this labyrinthine maze of human sorrow and joy, that I might become not a mere observer of the path of my fellow man, but a herald to show them the way. Will you lend me your wisdom, dear Marley, your detailed mandate no less, that I may learn to cast aside these shackles of worldliness and embrace the noble calling of kindness?"

Marley's ghost raised a hand to silence him, a pained gesture on his face as though even Marley was struggling mightily. "Ebenezer," he began, bearing the gravity of all eternity, "I come not of my own will, but at the behest of those who watch over mortal lives. Your journey of redemption, while admirable, is not yet complete."

Scrooge's brow furrowed. Why would Marley assert such a thing?

And why so suddenly? Scrooge was ready to embark on this most awkward quest, yet here was a specter telling him that even this would not suffice because first, he must work on his own self!

He had no tolerance for this!

"Not complete? But I have changed! I have given of my wealth and my time. The enigmatic figure of The Wanderer, shrouded in an air of solemnity and portent, bestowed upon me a sacred errand, one that bore upon its fragile shoulders the irrevocable fate of humanity itself. What more impactful deed can be placed on a lone man's shoulders? Yet you insist I must change, again?"

Marley's chains clinked as he moved closer.

His eyes, hollow yet piercing, bore into Scrooge's soul.

"You have indeed altered the trajectory of your mortal and simple existence, Ebenezer, and for that, you have found much grace. But redemption is not a solitary act, you see. The legacy you build must endure, not through deeds alone, but through the hearts and minds of those who come after you."

Scrooge sat heavily, his hand gripping the arm of his chair. A deep, aggrieved line appeared betwixt his eyes, a testament to the stubborn wrestling with the preeminent thorny problem within, hinting at both the mind's labor and the vexation it caused.

"Alas, I have not the faintest idea of what you speak. It is all nonsense to me, a deliberate puzzle. You speak in riddles, Jacob. Be clear! What must I do to secure this legacy you speak of?"

Marley's form wavered slightly, growing momentarily faint as though the effort of his presence were straining the bonds of his ethereal state. His voice was tinged by the weight of ages.

"You must become a guide, Ebenezer. Inspire the next generation, teach them to avoid the perilous pitfalls that ensnared us both. It is imperative that you find in yourself the sincere and true spirit of giving and accepting, for the soul of humanity hinges upon these sacred virtues, ensuring the flame of charity burns brightly long after you have taken your leave of this mortal coil."

This was worrying. This was desperate, unheard of!

He did not plan to take his leave from this mortal coil anytime soon, so why this … doubt?

"And what of you, Jacob?" Scrooge inquired, a softening, defeated note creeping into his tone; he was all out of fresh ideas to placate and sustain the poor specter which was itself bound in chains.

He just wanted it to take its leave. To be gone. He would make small talk meanwhile. "Why do you remain tethered to this world of shadows? Is there truly no hope for your release from such torment?"

Marley's gaze grew mournful, the sorrow of the ages reflecting in his eyes.

He replied, "My salvation, Ebenezer, lies intricately woven with your actions and those of all the living. You see, I depend on you! There exists a thread—an unbreakable connection—linking the departed to the realm of the living, through which the righteous deeds of the present can bring solace to the troubled souls of times gone by. If you fulfill your duty, if you foster a legacy of kindness and inspire others to embrace the enduring light of humanity, you may also help to liberate me from this eternal prison, shackled by my own misdeeds. Thus, it is I who stands upon the precipice of fortune, teetering, looking to you. Oh Scrooge, you must do your utmost, do the very best!"

Marley, the tormented spirit, gazed down on the spectral form hanging so wretchedly bound in chains of his own making, each clanking link a bitter reminder of the self-proclaimed misdeeds ensnaring him in perpetual sorrow's prison. For a fleeting instant, as the ethereal mist curled about him like tendrils of regret, he dared to entertain the tantalizing thought of liberation—of breaking free.

In short, he still aspired to taste the sweetness of grace that death had promised but not bestowed.

Scrooge's eyes widened, understanding, further daunted.

So here, too, was a poor soul entirely dependent on Scrooge's impending actions to set him free! Did the whole earth rely on him for its liberty? How was this remotely fair?

It was not. It simply could not be. It was unthinkable. Yet, here he was, taking on the task.

He smoothed back his unruly hair, then said quietly, "Then I shall do it, Jacob—not for your sake alone, but for the salvation of all who might suffer as we once did."

"Thank you," said the specter with a polite nod. "I should be most grateful if you would."

This was all very well but Scrooge still had received no actionable guidance. Alas, he would have to ask that infernal question yet again. He looked into Marley's eyes with a near deferential gaze.

"But first, pray, tell me, how shall I begin this momentous task?"

With a wave of his spectral hand, Marley conjured forth a faint luminescence, lighting the shadows as though whispering ancient secrets into the night. He leaned forward, conspiratorially.

"Well, it is obvious. You must seek out those who are lost and forlorn, Ebenezer," he whispered, tapping the side of his nose in a gesture as if to say, *hark, I am telling you a fine secret, a wisdom.*

"Mentor the young and guide the faltering, for within them lies the hope of our lineage. It is through the burgeoning hopes of the rising generation—those bright-eyed children who bear within them the potential to reshape the destiny of mankind—that we will effectuate the grand and noble alteration of our collective fate. These young souls, untainted by weary cynicism and the black dog of depression and woe so often clouding the hearts of their forebears, possess an innate vigor and a capacity for compassion. This, Ebenezer, can pierce through the thickest of veils obscuring our better selves.

"In their hands lies the promise of renewal and the power to cast aside the shackles of ignorance and injustice, leading us forth into a future resplendent with possibility, where the better angels of our nature may take flight. Use the wealth and wisdom bestowed upon you by fortune's fickle hand to sow seeds of kindness and understanding. Your influence shall ripple outward like the gentle waves of a tranquil sea, touching lives you may never even come to know. In doing so, you will be forging unbreakable bonds between ancestors and posterity. Between the living and the dead."

And so, that was the best answer coming to Scrooge: mentor the young.

Was that enough? It barely seemed so!

The chill of the room deepened, Marley's form beginning to wane, his presence being drawn away by an unknown force while also pulling down the atmosphere by the sheer gravity of his message.

Marley's voice was barely there by now, the faintest whistle as though brought in through the wind from between the trees, sending a frigid air around the room's periphery.

"Remember, dear Ebenezer," he cautioned. "Redemption is not merely a destination but a journey, a steadfast passage filled with obstacles, trials and triumphs. Walk the path with an unwavering heart, and the light of your efforts will shine across generations, guiding souls present and departed toward the promise of peace, harmony, gaiety, and celebration—the spirit of Christmas.

"Let love, compassion, and togetherness be the legacy you bestow, for in honoring this sacred relationship between the living and the dead, you shall ignite within both realms an enduring force for good that will carry through the ages."

As the ghost of Marley vanished into the ether as unexpectedly as it had appeared, the fire in the hearth flared brilliantly, casting brightness into the room's shadowy corners.

Scrooge sat in contemplative silence for a while, staring into space.

He now understood that his transformation was but the first step in a far greater mission, a vital link in the grand backdrop of existence binding together all souls, a sacred chain that intertwined the hearts of generations past, the living, and those yet to come.

In that peculiar stillness, his thoughts whirled, drawing him toward the profoundest truth of all ages: the stirring promise of Malachi 4:6, known to impart wisdom as ancient as the stars.

"And he shall turn the heart of the fathers to the children, and the heart of the children to their fathers, lest I come and smite the earth with a curse."

Oh, how his heart swelled at the notion that he, Ebenezer Scrooge, could be the fulcrum upon which the delicate balance of love and understanding might pivot!

Each father, a sentinel of past hopes and dreams, each child radiant in their future promise; what glorious harmony could arise from such alignment!

The specter of his dear departed mother, whom he had hardly known, flitted through his mind—would she, if indeed she might appear to him in this newfound state of grace, enfold him in a maternal embrace, bridging the chasm of their years apart?

A tender twinge ignited within his fluttering breast at the thought of seeing her face, and he could almost begin to imagine the depth of her kindly gaze, the unspoken love dwelling in each fleeting moment, the goodness denied him since birth to be rekindled by the embers of a purpose reborn.

In the depths of his contemplative reverie, Scrooge's thoughts turned as if drawn by an unseen hand to the figure of his father, that stern and formidable man whose heart had long been set in the iron vice of unyielding discontent. The man was the very embodiment of misery. Scrooge's childhood memories, rife with shadows of neglect and a father's frosty ruthlessness, unfolded like the dreary pages of a forgotten tome, a bitter history that had forged him into the man he now strove to renounce.

Yet, amidst the tempest of past grievances, a sliver of positivity ignited, envisioning a future transformed not just by his own metamorphosis, but also by a wildly ambitious, dreamlike imagining.

It was a dream that his acts of kindness and commemorations of the Christmas spirit might break through the granite veneer of his father's demeanor, a gentle spring thawing the harshest winter.

"Could it be," he mused, his heart racing with fervor, "that through the restorative power of love and giving, I might become the catalyst for change in that once-distant heart? Oh, what bliss it would be to lay aside the bitter legacy of resentment and forge a new relationship, father and son reunited not by the chains of their shared sorrow, but by the joyous bonds of mutual respect!"

He could almost perceive his father's burdensome spirit rising, becoming lifted, revealing beneath the scowling exterior an unquestionable tenderness borne not of fear, but of genuine love.

The kind of love and ardor that blossom when the icy grip of isolation relinquishes to the gentle embrace of community and empathy.

With such imaginings, Scrooge felt newly fueled by conviction; he could transform not merely his own destiny, but also the heritage of his family, ensuring that affection's tender roots could tunnel their way deep into the future, nurturing generations yet unborn.

And what of his beloved nephew Fred? Yes, that darling soul had also departed, but Scrooge still dearly wished to make peace with how he had once behaved toward this wonderful blessing of a man.

The vivid image of the young man—so full of life, laughter, and enveloping warmth—bloomed to life like the first flower of spring after a long, severe winter. How often he had shunned Fred's earnest invitations, hurling back the joys of family connection with all the jaded indifference of a heart wrapped in ice! If only he might rekindle that relationship; he could imagine it making peace within his tormented heart, this wondrous imagining filling him with jubilant expectation. To share Christmas cheer with Fred, to laugh and to celebrate the bonds of kinship that should never have frayed …

Could there be any greater embodiment of love and renewal?

The designs of the heart, it seemed, were capable of working in wondrous ways, enabling him to become the architect of a deeply compassionate legacy.

Reminiscing about his beloved Fred, Scrooge's thoughts drifted inexorably toward his cherished sister, Fan, a luminous, effervescent spirit whose playful laughter had once danced through the halls of his memory like sunlight filtering through autumn leaves.

Ah, Fan! With her bright countenance and gentle heart, she had been the embodiment of love in a household marred by meanness, her kindness a balm brought to him to soothe the raw edges of his childhood unhappiness. He could almost hear her dulcet voice as sweet as a nursery chime, calling him forth with tender urgings. "Come, Brother! Come share in the joy!"

He imagined Fred again standing before him too, a living testament to her extraordinary legacy, inviting him not only to rekindle their bond but also to honor the spirit of Fan herself.

What if, through the celebration of Christmas spirit and familial affection, Scrooge might somehow bridge the void that fate itself had unkindly severed? The prospect brought a swell of emotion, the tantalizing hope of reuniting with her soul in some heavenly realm, the anguished confines of life and death surrendering to the boundless horizon of love.

"Oh, sweet and unyielding Fan," he uttered, sighing. "Might we meet again beyond these earthly cares, in the realm where love conquers all, where the hearts of brothers and sisters do not merely beat, but harmonize as one?" In that moment, he resolved to honor her memory and the bond she had fostered between them, knowing that through his transformation, he might finally embody the generous spirit she had so lovingly striven to cultivate in life.

Flames danced merrily in the hearth as though they, too, had discovered this new vigor, the shadows that had once lain like a pall over his life cast aside by the brilliance of understanding.

"Yes, I shall embrace this journey with fervor," he declared to the empty room, his voice ringing out. "I shall honor the love of those who walked before me and nurture the hearts of those who follow after. With each act of charity and magnanimous gesture, I will forge bonds unbroken, weaving a richness of sentiment transcending time itself, forever entwining the hearts of the living and the dead."

Chapter 7: A Fine Legacy

When the first rays of morning's sun pierced the frost-laden windows of Ebenezer Scrooge's home, they alighted upon a man whose heart was still brimming with purpose anew.

With resolve unshakeable and the lingering throes of The Wanderer and Marley's ghostly warnings still playing, Scrooge rose, driven by a profound sense of need.

If the spirit of Christmas and its many virtues he had embraced were to endure, he must get out and sow the seeds of kindness and moral resolve in the hearts of the young.

Without that, there was nothing, for they were the ones destined to inherit the world.

Yet, amidst this burgeoning zeal, there lingered a curious neglect within his thoughts; the hour had come upon him in stealth, masking the jubilant proclamation of the day.

It was, contrary to his initial surmise, not merely the dawn of another trivial morning, but the revered celebration of Christmas Day itself.

The realization struck him like a tempest, awakening memories of hearth and home, of tinkling laughter shared amongst kin, goodwill and good humor amongst all people permeating the air.

How could he, a man newly kindled in spirit, have allowed such a momentous occasion to slip unacknowledged through his fingers? The ghosts of yesteryear constantly surged up from within him, so why had they not reminded him with tender insistence that this day, rich with the promise of renewal and joy, was imminent, and at the core of all he had come to cherish?

"I shall not be the one to sever this precious welding link between generations, forged by this day's resplendent spirit," he uttered to himself, his voice overtaken by a fervor.

His thoughts took a dear turn toward Fred's children.

Since Fred's untimely passing, Scrooge had often visited Lily and the little ones, hoping to provide whatever comfort he could muster. Scrooge felt a profound sense of duty, prompting him to swiftly take upon himself the sacred charge of providing for Lily and her little ones. It was a testament to his reclaimed heart, that the comfort and security of his nephew's widow and orphans became, without delay, his most earnest and cherished concern.

Yet now, he perceived his role in their lives as something immensely grander. The children, innocent and tender, were standing at the threshold of life's myriad temptations, and it was upon him to shepherd them. Under his watchful gaze, they would become torchbearers of compassion, bearing the light in a society increasingly mired in selfish ambition.

The decision made, Scrooge wasted no time.

Wrapping himself in a thick woolen coat, scarf, and gloves, he collected the children's presents and set forth through frosted streets; the crisp air nipped at his cheeks, yet the clarity of his mission infused each step with purpose, propelling him into the heart of London, its streets filled with seasonal cheer.

As he ventured forth, the streets were alight, bedecked in garlands of holly and ivy, their vibrant greens a jubilant contrast against the wintry white blanketing the ground.

Shop windows sparkled with lights like stars plummeted to earth, and within, cheerful displays of toys and trinkets beckoned to passersby with the promise of delight.

Hearty laughter and merry carols floated through the air.

The steam rising from vendors' carts laden with roasted chestnuts and sweet confections also invoked a positively intoxicating aura of honeyed homeliness.

Amidst the bustling throng, children darted about with uncontainable glee, their cheeks aglow with excitement as they reveled in the plethora of gifts bestowed upon them.

With rosy faces framed by bright woolen hats, they stumbled chuckling through the snow, their laughter ringing like bells, tiny hands clutching dolls draped in bright ribbons. Wooden soldiers stood at attention, eager for the day's grand adventures. The air was filled with shouts of joy as they chased one another in a frenetic game of tag, their breath misting in the frosty air, mingling with the season's.

Scrooge paused a moment, allowing the joyous symphony of voices and laughter to wash over him; it felt as though he were witnessing a world lit not merely by this day's brightness, but also by the radiant glow of happiness. It struck him, then, wasn't this the embodiment of Christmas spirit itself?

Wasn't this what he was striving for, to bring this experience to all children and all of mankind that he could reach? Yes! His mission was to cultivate in the hearts of children what it meant to know togetherness and love, something he himself had once cruelly denied, ensuring it could never again be extinguished, thus withheld from him too.

He was aglow at the thought of being a part of this grand celebration, sharing in its laughter, its immense joy, and above all, the kindness perfusing the air like the sweetest aroma of cinnamon.

With a heart as light as the tumbling snowflakes, Scrooge pressed on through the city.

Christmas Day promised so much more than mere merriment—it offered the chance for rebirth, for reconciliation. Yet, as he gazed upon the merriment that enveloped him—children laughing, families embracing, strangers offering smiles like gifts—a weighty thought descended, a specter determined to linger in the recesses of his mind. He reminded himself of how the multiplicity of stark realities still gripped many of the city's denizens, considering the relentless march of industrial greed and the cold indifference of a world too often blinded to how it had caused its own suffering.

The image of hungry mouths and forlorn faces haunted him; a dire fate was awaiting his beloved city should he fail to fulfill his mission.

These sights, though harrowing to behold, only instilled a great need, a stronger indomitable drive to liberate London from the grip of avarice and rekindle a true atmosphere of cheer.

Each of his steps was now steeped in purpose; the joy surrounding him—that radiant, enchanting, inimitable gladness—could only flourish if nurtured by humankind's great fraternity.

***

Eventually, after what felt like a walk of a day and a half, he found himself arriving at Fred's modest abode. Indeed, despite the obvious and deeply distressing awareness that Fred was no longer on this earthly plane, this was a place he still considered Fred's and always would, for the rest of his days.

Every wall, flower, timber strut, gate or paving stone screamed out, *I was Fred's, you know.*

Fred, who is no more.

Fred, your nephew, that bright spirit who laughed, who hugged, who extended a hand to all of mankind ... Fred, the one whose hearty invitations you did eschew, preferring your own sad company.

Scrooge felt so much guilt, so much ... sorrow. So much regret for the times past, ones in which he had wallowed in miserly oneness, alone, hidden away, refusing to greet the world and answer the door.

Dearest Fred. Where had he traveled to? Was his spirit at peace in the next place, and did he look down upon the efforts of his uncle, approving of each endeavor? Did he? Scrooge could only hope so.

If not, or if Fred did not think he was trying his utmost, giving his all, then he would have failed.

Despite Scrooge's descending morose demeanor, he was thankfully soon met with gleeful exuberance by the children, their spirits unmarred by the somber realities of the world.

Young Edward, whose bright eyes mirrored his father's, sparkling like baubles delicately placed throughout the welcoming branches of the prickly pine tree, tugged eagerly at Scrooge's coat fabric.

His small fingers almost trembled with excitement as he drew himself in close, whispering of the treasures lying waiting for them, gifts wrapped in vibrant paper that glistened by cozy candlelight.

"Look, Uncle Scrooge!" he exclaimed, pointing with a childish fervor toward the corner where a modest array of toys stood as a tribute to the season's bounty, a remnant of Fred's unyielding practicality. He had been ever vigilant in the art of thrift, preserving gifts far ahead in his dutiful preparations for the much-anticipated season of goodwill to all men.

Little Emmeline, innocent yet curious, peered shyly from behind her mother's skirts, round cheeks flushed with anticipation. *Ah, delightful Emmy ... she hardly ever seems to age, always a little cherubic child, pink-skinned and chubby, vivid blue eyes always instilled with such immense surprise!*

It was as though she had landed in the world from a strange place far away, that she knew not of the customs and habits here and would make her pretty eyes widen at every small thing she beheld.

With each passing moment, her timid nature gave way to the thrill of the day, for she was enchanted by the sound of jangling bells and the aroma of delectable wafting treats, making her all but set aside the entire world beyond the threshold. "Will there be a feast for us, Mama?" she asked quietly, her voice a sweet whisper tinged with excitement. She tugged at her mother's apron. "Will there, Mama?"

Lily, pallid and looking increasingly frail beneath the heavy mantle of still undissipated grief, felt Fred's absence with an aching sharpness on this day, one they had cherished with tender esteem.

She managed to greet Scrooge with warmth regardless, putting on an air of happiness for the children's sake, and because her heart was woven with pleasure and trust for the man who once had shunned them stubbornly and perpetually. She observed her children with a mix of sorrow and joy, marveling at how the spirit of Christmas had the uncanny ability to uplift hearts and lighten souls, even in the face of an undeniably immense loss. The walls of their humble home sparkled with decorations crafted by tiny hands, garlands of cranberries and popcorn strung with love; their laughter filled every nook and cranny, turning the modest space into a sanctuary brimming with affection.

"Come, Uncle Scrooge!" Edward called out, his infectious enthusiasm beckoning Scrooge into family's everlasting festive embrace. "You must see what Father Christmas has brought us! There's a new game, and I want to show you how it works!"

A growing sense of pride and delight made him puff out his chest at the prospect of sharing their joy, almost as if he had raised this nurturing, loving family by himself.

Amidst the remnants of his former self lay the promise of a sparkling new beginning, a chance to weave himself into the fabric of their lives and to play a role they so desperately craved.

"Uncle Ebenezer," Lily whispered, her voice tired yet hopeful, "what brings you here so early?"

Kneeling to meet her inquisitive gaze, Scrooge answered Lily's question as he allowed his voice to take on a gentle yet firm tone. "Why, I come bearing lessons, my dear Lily. Lessons of life, of kindness, and of the sacred duty we owe to one another. Particularly now, at this time of the year."

The children exchanged curious glances, puzzlement quickly giving way to eager anticipation.

Lily gestured for them to gather by the comforting hearth.

With all the spirited enthusiasm of a young bird taking its first flight, Emmeline danced into Scrooge's lap, her eyes sparkling as she settled herself with a charming familiarity.

Eager to absorb the wisdom he had to impart, she nestled closely against him, bestowing on him a cascade of affection. Her delighted presence was a testament to the bond that had blossomed anew between them, for in that tender moment, the layers of loss melted away, leaving only the pure joy of connection. She regarded him with the warmth and trust of a daughter seeing her father for the first time in months of absence, a delight not easily matched by any other treasure the world had to offer.

It was there in the parlor, with the smoky fire casting a warm glow upon their faces, that Scrooge began to weave a tale both captivating and profound. With vivid detail and the fervor of a storyteller, he recounted to them that monumental night on which the spirits had visited, the tumultuous journey from avarice to renewal, and the exalted joy subsequently uncovered in selfless giving.

Although the children had heard this delightful tale recounted on previous occasions—after all, it was tradition now—their eager little faces radiated a rapturous attentiveness, as if it were the first time they had been graced with the pleasure of its telling. Each word spinning forth from Scrooge's lips fell upon their ears like a cherished melody, inviting them into a world where dreams danced in the glimmering light of imagination. They sat, wide-eyed and breathlessly still, drinking in the syllables, with hearts alight and spirits soaring, savoring the magic that transformed the humble room into a realm of wonder and enchantment. The familiarity of the story only heightened their delight.

They knew that within those cherished phrases lay the promise of laughter, adventure, and the joyous spirit so beautifully and exquisitely adorning the season.

Thus, they hung upon every tale, cherishing each moment as if it were a precious Yule gift.

Soon, he added something else to bring delight to their faces.

"I have a new tale to share this year, one freshly experienced," he began, lifting a finger with the earnest gravity befitting a man recounting the most paramount of truths. "Both new and old specters together came to see me in the twilight of my slumbers last night; a being called The Wanderer, alongside my departed partner, the distinguished Mr. Marley, graced me with his ethereal presence."

"Why, Uncle Scrooge?" little Emmy dared to ask. "What made them come to you?"

"Well," he said, "Marley wished to impart upon me a noble charge, you see, an instruction to weave the wondrous spirit of Christmas deep into the fabric of London Town, and ensure it stays."

Scrooge paused, deeply engrossed in reverie. Those who gathered about him leaned closer, their breath mingling with the fragrant warmth of the hearth. Indeed, it was not merely a mission but a sacred undertaking—a divinely inspired quest, if he may be so bold—for he harbored within him a fervent desire to ignite the hearts of the young ones encircling him, so dear to his soul.

With every twinkle of excitement in their bright eyes, a surge of purpose was welling up inside him, a determination to scatter the bitter cobwebs of mankind's insolent and grievous ignorance, and making ample room for a warmth robust enough to envelop even the most frostbitten spirits.

Edward, particularly enthralled by Scrooge's tale, listened intently, entranced by the spectral visitations and their haunting warnings. Timid little Emmeline, emboldened by her brother's rapture, hesitantly asked, "But were you scared, Uncle? I know I would be scared."

"Quite the contrary, my dear. I was comforted." Laughter was in his voice as he continued, "It taught me that to live without love and charity is no true life at all."

***

As the days flitted past, elusive and ungraspable, Scrooge's daily visits became the highlights of the children's young lives. He taught them the value inherent in small acts of sharing: dividing a loaf of bread to share with a neighbor in need; tending to the ailing; or offering comfort to a friend beset by sorrow. Most importantly, he imparted to them the wisdom of keeping their father's memory alive by living just as he had, with a heart open to the struggles of others, offering support.

But Scrooge's mission extended far beyond the confines of Fred's family.

He sought out other young souls gone adrift in life's tumultuous sea, whose dreams were but sparks beneath harsh winds of circumstance. In London's bustling streets, he discovered orphans huddling together for warmth, their faces pinched with hunger and need. He encountered apprentices toiling beneath the oppressive weight of toil, youthful hopes all but crushed by unrelenting labor.

To these children, Scrooge became a mentor, a friend, an ally.

He orchestrated gatherings in which stories were shared, songs filled the air, and simple meals nourished not just the body but the spirit too. During those evenings, he spoke of unity and empathy, urging the young to recognize themselves not as isolated individuals, but as integral threads woven into a vast and grand embroidery. "Every seemingly insignificant act of kindness you perform," he declared with heartfelt intensity, "is a stitch to strengthen and serve the whole."

Particularly special to Scrooge was young Tom, whose boundless curiosity and infectious spirit shone out, throwing into brightness the corners of his world with the brilliance of a thousand stars.

In the young boy's eyes, Scrooge perceived he was seeing so much promise, untamed potential eager to stretch for the skies, ready to unfold in the warm light of spring.

It was not merely a scholarly pursuit that Scrooge envisioned for the boy; rather, he sought to nurture within Tom the qualities that would enable him to flourish as a respected and productive member of society, as well as a true shepherd of charity and goodwill toward others.

With each passing day, Tom's spirit soared higher, emboldened by a sense of progress.

To the noble end he kept in mind, Scrooge set forth a plan embracing both knowledge and character-building. They would meet in the cozy study of Scrooge's own home, adorned simply yet invitingly.

With a stack of books—some old and dog-eared, others bright and new—he encouraged Tom to explore the vast realms of literature, history, and the sciences, believing that through broad learning, the boy's world would expand beyond the restrictive confines of his station.

Within the vibrant heart of young Tom, Scrooge perceived a stirring ambition, a vision that might one day see him stride into the hallowed halls of political clout, not as a mere player in the grand game but as a crusader on behalf of the poor and destitute, a tireless advocate for justice and reform. A people's champion!

It was a prospect that thrilled the marrow of Scrooge's bones, for he envisioned Tom wielding both the quill and the principles of justice with equal fervor, crafting laws and regulations that would uplift the downtrodden and mend the tattered fabric of society.

Scrooge imagined the boy confronting the sordid ills of the world with a conviction able to burn brighter than any energy source, a bold champion for those whose voices had long been silenced by indifference and cruelty. As they delved into the tomes filling the study's shelves, Scrooge imparted to Tom not just knowledge but equally, a profound sense of duty to look beyond the self.

Tom should champion the cause of humanity, igniting the hope that one day, he might rise as a harbinger of change in a world too often covered in negativity and disparity.

"Tom, my lad," Scrooge would say, his eyes twinkling, "the written word is a key unlocking the gates to countless ideas. In these pages lies the knowledge of centuries! Let us embark on a journey."

Thus, they would delve into stories, Tom finding himself amidst the thrilling adventures of valiant knights and noble quests, which Scrooge would artfully weave into lessons on virtue, righteousness, and integrity. Scrooge, with a paternal air and an earnestness that bespoke his deep affection for the art of the tale, turned Tom's attention to one of his own most cherished novels, *Oliver Twist*.

He spoke with fervor of young Oliver, a boy who, though born into the bleakest of misfortunes, triumphed over the snares of crime and the shadow of desperation, finding hope and redemption amidst the dire and unyielding trials of poverty and human frailty. Then, ever eager to impart wisdom through literature, he next turned to *Pride and Prejudice*, delving into its themes of class mobility and the follies of prejudice, highlighting the oppressive boundaries erected by society's rigid hierarchies.

He even ventured into the dark and thought-provoking realms of Mary Shelley's *Frankenstein*, drawing parallels to teach Tom the grave consequences of unbridled ambition, alongside the moral responsibilities that must accompany any and every pursuit of scientific knowledge.

After reading about a brave hero's selfless deeds, Scrooge would set Tom pondering deep moral questions. "Tell me, dear boy," he would prompt, "what does courage mean to you? And how might one act, not merely for oneself, but for others? What does it mean to be generous of heart?"

In such manner, he nourished Tom's ability to empathize and reflect, encouraging him to understand the struggles of those around. They would often venture into the streets together, where Scrooge would guide Tom through the teeming markets and bustling lanes.

Scrooge would stop to converse with the vendors, the beggars, and even the workmen, demonstrating the importance of kindness and recognition of each person's contribution in life.

"See that fellow?" Scrooge gestured toward a stonemason laboring in the midday sun, beads of sweat glistening on his brow. "He works tirelessly for the wellbeing of his family. Let us offer him a few coins and a word of encouragement! A small gesture such as this can lift the heaviest heart."

Tom watched intently, standing by the wayside as Scrooge approached the man with sincere words of praise for his craftsmanship, handing over a few shillings with a friendly smile.

The joy in the mason's eyes was an indelible lesson for Tom, who began to grasp the weight and power of unconditional giving, a foundational guiding principle.

Tom was not the only young soul upon whom Scrooge bestowed his careful attentions and boundless hopes; rather, his heart, now encouraged by the many shows of kindness he had long denied himself, embraced a gathering of spirited youths, all eager to learn and grow beneath the gentle tutelage of a man known to have once been lost in labyrinthine willful ignorance.

Scrooge developed artistic pursuits for them to share, believing creativity to be a wellspring from which goodness could freely and plentifully flow. One dreary afternoon, as the rain fell softly, Scrooge gathered his merry band of eager children under his thoughtful wing, introducing them to the enchanting realm of painting and drawing. Palettes arrayed before them like splendid treasures, he urged these spirited youngsters to turn their eyes toward the city.

They were to take heed of the silent, overlooked souls ambling past them daily, their stories rich with unspoken struggles and unrelated dreams.

As brushes stroked canvas, each child learned to observe the world with freshness, discovering not only the exquisite beauty of their surroundings but also the profound worth encapsulated within each individual life, a luminous truth becoming bolder with each stroke of color.

"Paint not just what you see, Tom," Scrooge advised, guiding the boy's hand, "but what you feel. Let your canvas reflect your heart's desires, the compassion igniting hope in the hearts of others."

In the golden glow of a late afternoon sun, filtering through the tattered curtains of Scrooge's humble abode, the old man gathered the children together once more.

Their eyes were sparking with anticipation. Today, the air was infused with the sweet promise of music, a captivating art form that could transport the spirit to realms sublime and divine.

With an array of neglected instruments strewn about—a battered piano, a few weathered violins, and a curious assortment of old flutes—Scrooge took it upon himself to unveil the sacred power of melody. "Gather around, my joyful charges!" he proclaimed, a twinkle in his eye. "For music is no mere pastime; it is the very prayer of the righteous, the profoundest mode of human expression, and an instrument through which our souls may commune with the heavens!"

As he lovingly placed his gnarled fingers on the piano keys, the first notes rang out, a tinkling cascade filling the air with a warmth reminiscent of sunbeams piercing through dark clouds.

Within a few, tentative notes, a familiar melody emerged, a melody that, like a ghost of Christmases past, instantly awakened a profound sense of nostalgia in the hearts of the children.

It was, of course, that timeless hymn, *Silent Night*, its haunting beauty stirring within them peace and wonder. The children watched, enraptured, their hearts swelling as the room thrilled with the rich concoction of sounds. Each note seemed to weave a delicate bond among them, a shared understanding transcending their youthful innocence.

With patience and passion, Scrooge taught them not only to play but also to feel, the rhythm of a somber waltz echoing life's trials. The jubilant burst of a lively jig reflected the many facets of joy that life could bestow. "Feel the music in your bones, dear children, for it is alive! A vessel of our hopes, our sorrows, and our triumphs. In its embrace, you shall find the voice of your own spirit."

As they took turns instrumentalizing their hearts' desires, each child discovered a unique language within their created symphonies. Little Mary, with her delicate fingers, conjured up a sweet lullaby whispering of dreams and quiet wishes, while boisterous Jake unleashed a raucous tune to celebrate all the coarseness and hilarity of youth. With each rising crescendo and sweet diminuendo, they learned that music was not merely an arrangement of notes, but also a reflection of themselves, a potent reminder that they, too, had stories worthy of telling to young and old.

As the enchanting melodies filled the room, Scrooge, mischief in his eyes, rose from his seat, hurriedly beckoning the children to join him in joyous frolic.

"Ah, my merry little friends! Music yearns not only to be heard but also to be experienced in every fiber of our being!" He took the lead, guiding them in a lively dance that twirled and spun like the notes.

Each child, giggling and stumbling, found their happy rhythm, feet tapping and arms waving as they embraced the exuberance of life. Laughter mingled with the music, and in that vibrant whirl of skirts and laughter, they discovered not merely a series of steps, but a joyous liberation—a celebration of their spirits intertwined, an affirmation that in dancing, as in music, they could share their hearts and souls with the world, reveling in the sheer, unadulterated pleasure of being alive.

As dusk painted the sky in shades of indigo and gold, Scrooge beamed with pride at his little ensemble, each child a gleaming star. They made merry in a cosmic array, spirits harmonizing in a glorious chorus of life's myriad colors, twirling and leaping with youth's incomparable vivacity.

The children's footsteps, as loud and clattering as they occasionally could be, nevertheless offered a jubilant testament to the joy of existence. It was so wonderful to be a child in these times!

The lightness of each child's rhythmic feet attested to the glee in their young souls, at least for a short time freed from the dread and cold fear of being worked to death or left to starve someday.

Scrooge was infinitely proud to have been the instigator of this merriment.

Thus, the lesson of music became more than an art—it transformed into a prayer, a siren call to the goodness within all men, reminding them that in each note played with sincerity, a divine truth lay waiting to be discovered. Scrooge, once a solitary figure, now was standing tall amidst a radiant gathering of young hearts, their laughter ringing out, sounding through the ages; it was a testament to their newfound understanding that love, music, and the stories of every soul were forever intertwined.

Scrooge's keen gaze, sharp as the frost-laden air of a winter's eve, narrowed upon young Tom with a scrutiny that seemed to pierce through the boy's spirit. His eyes, long ago clouded by the weight of avarice and discontent, now demonstrated a level of understanding profoundly familiar.

It was as if he were seeking to unravel the threads of Tom's youthful boisterousness, to gauge the depth of the joy reflected in the lad's countenance. Scrooge, his creased brow a map of his former life, wondered at the amazing metamorphosis taking place before him.

One of the most profound lessons Scrooge imparted to Tom was structured around acts of charity during the festive season. Together, they organized a small gathering for the less fortunate in a neighborhood community hall, filling the space with laughter, music, and warm food, a feast promising to nourish the bellies as well as the hearts of those who attended. Scrooge involved Tom in every step, from planning and preparations to serving meals with an open hand and wide, warm smile.

"Remember, Tom," he would say gently as they ladled hearty soup into bowls, "the spirit of giving is not to be confined to the holiday season; it is a seed we plant, to be nurtured and shared throughout the year, on every day. Look into the eyes of those you serve; therein lies our true purpose."

As the sunlight danced on the snow in the weeks leading to yet another Christmas, Scrooge orchestrated a small exhibition of the children's artwork, inviting neighbors and friends to witness the beauty emergent when hearts and minds were able to be nurtured by sincerity and kindness.

Tom stood contentedly by his own creations, cheeks flushed with excitement, though also with the mild embarrassment typical of shy youth as Scrooge beamed with paternal pride.

"You see, my young Tom," he said before the gathered crowd, "art is a powerful vessel for good. Let your heart be the artist, create life with kindness, and let each stroke bring love to the world."

And so, through winter's chill, Scrooge continued pouring himself into the young boy, nurturing a student alongside a man who would carry forth the spirit of goodwill into the world.

After months of toil this year, during which he had labored with a zeal arising from his reformed spirit, Scrooge's efforts began bearing fruit, much to his astonishment and delight.

The children he had embraced—the once neglected and overlooked souls adrift in the bustling currents of the city—now radiated a renewed vitality so palpable that it caught the bewildered attention of their bemused parents. Whispers of transformation unfurled through the smoky streets.

Tales were woven about disengaged children once driven to shuffle like shadows through the alleys, who were now bursting forth through doorways, peals of irrepressible laughter ringing out.

Emboldened by their enthusiasm, Scrooge extended the embrace of his grand plan to their parents, inviting them—a band of eager allies—into the sun-drenched promise of new beginnings.

The once-humble lodgings previously sounding only with the clattering of coins were now thrumming with laughter and jubilation as families gathered, sharing heartfelt stories, earnest ideas, and a newfound sense of interconnectedness to knit them tighter than the finest cotton.

This delightful metamorphosis did not escape the keen eye of Bob Cratchit.

His heart, though burdened by the weight of his own struggles, was buoyed by the uplifting sight of his own beloved Tim, his spirit soaring with enjoyment.

"Father, look!" Tim would exclaim, his frame almost alight with life as he joined in the merriment, casting aside the somber cloak of illness once marring a sickly frame and face.

Driven by an irrepressible fount of curiosity, parents soon found themselves irresistibly drawn to Scrooge's door, eager to uncover the secret behind this remarkable change. Many had been compelled there by the sight of Tim, who, despite frailties, was swiftly becoming an emblem of infectious joy.

As he stood amidst the growing circle of Christmas spirit seekers, with young Tim by his side—the boy's sturdy arm draped over Scrooge's shoulder in a gesture of trust and affection—Scrooge guided the parents' steps and uplifted their spirits. His heart swelled, warmed by the tender pride long believed to have been lost and buried beneath the weight of the years.

Gazing at the radiant faces surrounding him—Bob's beaming countenance as he looked on with gratitude and admiration, and Tim, the indomitable angel, standing as a towering testament to trials so valiantly surmounted, his presence bringing a great sense of resilience—Scrooge dreamed that perhaps, before he joined the ethereal spirits who had so profoundly moved him, he could indeed create a lasting harmony of goodwill to encourage generations to come.

Word of Scrooge's noble efforts began to ripple through the neighborhood.

Some of his erstwhile business associates scoffed, branding his endeavors mere sentimental folly. Yet others, moved by his sincerity and the palpable impact of his work, rallied to his cause cautiously. Together, they established funds to support education for the impoverished and workshops to teach practical skills, instilling dignity and self-respect within the beleaguered young citizens of London.

As another Christmas drew near, Scrooge surveyed the city with a heart brimming with fulfillment.

The work ahead remained substantial, yet he perceived in the eyes of those he mentored a glimpse of the world for which he had been yearning, one bathed in kindness, in which no one was destined to struggle alone. And so, with a heart full and a purpose resolute, Ebenezer Scrooge pressed on, occasionally whispering into the wind, "This is for you, Fred, my dear boy, never forgotten."

Chapter 8: Battle for the Future

London, shrouded in the smog of industry, was a city caught in the grip of transformation.

Steam engines roared, factories belched smoke into the heavens, and progress marched forward with a relentless stride. Yet, amidst this clamor of innovation came murmurs of dissent, whispers of resentment toward one man whose ideals stood starkly against the tide of greed and exploitation.

This latest development had always been coming to Scrooge but had taken its time, and now, finally, Ebenezer Scrooge found himself cast as a figure of contention among the city's elite.

His charitable endeavors, though widely celebrated by the common folk, were viewed by the powerful as a disruption to the natural order of profit and power.

Men of industry, their fortunes growing with each passing day, began to see Scrooge not as a redeemed philanthropist but as a meddlesome obstacle to their dominion over the city.

The conflict came to a head when Scrooge announced a new initiative, a series of educational workshops aimed at teaching the children of London's poorest neighborhoods the values of empathy and cooperation, as well as practical skills to help them navigate life's harshest realities.

Funded entirely by Scrooge's personal wealth, it was lauded by the working class but was drawing ceaseless sharp criticism from those who saw it as an affront to their interests.

While Scrooge was succeeding in changing the currents of London, seemingly defeating the insidious demons of ignorance and want that had long shackled his fellow citizens, there brewed an undercurrent of treachery among those whose interests lay in the relentless pursuit of gold and silver.

These industrious magnates, with their slicked-back hair and clad in the finest fabrics that money could procure, convened in the dimly lit halls of their clandestine assembly, plotting with the cunning of seasoned foxes intent on securing their own fortunes.

At the head of this nefarious gathering stood Mr. Blackthorn, the prominent factory owner, whose name inspired fear and admiration in equal measure.

His voice, unfettered by the impasses of morality, rang out with chilling authority, cutting through the viscous black miasma of smoke and ambition.

"Gentlemen," he began with ire and spittle, "we find ourselves at a perilous crossroads. A man of influence, that meddling reprobate Scrooge, no less, dares trifle with our dominion! He seeks to enlighten the masses, to rob our control, our hard-won prosperity! What say ye?"

Murmurs of disgruntlement swept far and wide through the assembly, each member's countenance reflecting discontent and anxiety. "Can you believe that the witless fool thinks he can redeem the scoundrel of the street, the common man," said Mr. Grayson, weaselly and with a penchant for deceit. "How quaint! But in his softness lies opportunity, a vulnerability we must exploit! And what say ye?"

A cheer rose to the skies at this too.

Blackthorn, nodding sagely, turned to face his brothers-in-arms.

"Indeed, you speak wisely, Grayson. We have our ears to the ground, and I have heard whispers concerning a particular affection that Scrooge harbors for a lad named Tom. A most unseemly 'tender' affection, if I am not mistaken, one that could serve our purposes most advantageously."

"Tom, is it?" piped up Mrs. Dobbins, the only woman among them, her sharp tongue rumored to slice through flesh as easily as she could cut through textiles. "That wretched boy who narrowly escaped the callous clutches of the workhouse! Put a strain upon that bond, and perhaps we can rattle the foundations of Scrooge's heart. He is but a man, after all, and all men have a breaking point—"

"Oh, let us be careful, Mrs. Dobbins!" warned Mr. Pemberton, characterized by his fussy demeanor and spectacles sliding down his nose. "We should tread lightly. Scrooge is more formidable than he appears. Let us not underestimate the depths of that man's cheek and tenacity."

"Fear not," Mr. Blackthorn assured, his dark demeanor underpinned by ambition. "Our intentions shall remain shrouded in the mantle of discretion. We will plant the seeds of doubt, subtly inflaming the boy's ties to his benefactor, until the thread frays to the point of rupture.

"Naught but a whisper here, a calculated move there, and I swear he will crumble before us! Imagine it, gentlemen! The masses, destabilized and forlorn, will look to us their steadfast saviors, reaping a harvest of influence and power to bask in the light of our most coveted desires."

The room seized, the air curdled with conspiratorial fervor and the silent promise of yet more riches to come. And thus, in the shadows of industry and greed, the plot had been woven in ambition and spite. This scheme could very well prove the undoing of Ebenezer Scrooge, a man whose heart, though warmed anew, stood in grave peril from those thriving on the back of devious, nefarious acts.

***

In a more sinister corner of London, within the opulent chambers adorned with gilded trappings that bespoke the mayor's considerable wealth and influence, Mr. Blackthorn paced with an air of unrestrained ambition. The mayor, his rotund figure swathed in draperies bulging under their own extravagance and the weight of too many fine dinners, lounged before an imposing desk cluttered with papers detailing numerous contracts enticingly beneficial to both men.

They were, after all, kindred spirits of enterprise, united in their unscrupulousness.

"Your Lordship, allow me to present to you an opportunity most splendid," Blackthorn began, his voice smooth as honey but laden with the bitter undertones of constraint. "It revolves around our esteemed neighbor, Mr. Scrooge, that unassailable buffoon who dares meddle in the affairs of our industry and nurture a company of children. A cohort, I fear, that could threaten our society."

The mayor, his brow furrowing slightly, leaned in, eager to catch the wicked current of the scheme.

"Indeed, the man's charitable pursuits have ruffled feathers, particularly among our esteemed business circles. If you're suggesting a means of rendering him impotent, consider me intrigued."

A mischievous smile, akin to the sort of grin one might expect from a sly fox that had just laid eyes upon a flock of unsuspecting chickens, crept slowly across the unscrupulous administrator's face.

As his eyes, those keen and calculating orbs, narrowed to slits, one could almost hear the silent cogs of ambition grinding in the shadowy recesses of his mind.

He sat poised, scarcely able to contain his bubbling excitement, acting to all eyes like a child on the brink of unveiling an elaborate prank upon unsuspecting peers.

As Mr. Blackthorn observed the mayor's keen interest transforming into palpable eagerness, a most unwelcome yet irresistible glee suffused his wily demeanor.

The mayor, whose rotund form wobbled with unbridled ambition and the pursuit of substance, leaned in closer, eager and giddy eyes wide with anticipation. It was not mere curiosity that shone within those shifty orbs, but also a scheming desire, the rumbling hunger for conspiratorial gain.

Feeling the gravity of this pivotal moment—the threads of his nefarious plot hanging tantalizingly in the air as a fruit longing for plucking—Mr. Blackthorn began to rub his hands together in a gesture both reflexive and deliberate, a subtle manifestation of the delight welling within.

The motion produced a soft, conspiratorial whisper, echoing with malevolent promise, as if to say that fortune and influence were now within their grasp, awaiting seizure by soft and eager hands.

"Ah, Lord Mayor," he began, his voice a silken murmur. "You see before you not merely an ambitious man, but also the custodian of an extraordinary scheme destined to reshape the landscape of our fair city and grant us both untold wealth and respect! Allow me to unfold the splendid tapestry I have woven, a design most cunning, whereupon our less scrupulous adversary, Mr. Scrooge, might find himself ensnared in a net of scandal and ruin! We shall strike at his Achilles' heel, that tender spot, that sentimental weakness for the wretched urchin, Tom. That ragamuffin, a waif of the streets, shall be our instrument of retribution, a poisoned dart aimed at the heart of his afflicted soul."

As he spoke, the lights dimmed and brightened in quick succession, the shadows lengthening as if the walls themselves were leaning in to listen.

His fervent proclamation ignited the air with an electric thrill, sending shivers of anticipation across the room. Blackthorn's imagination was running riot, conjuring vivid images of triumph, glittering coins, and whispers of admiration from a deeply envious society. Soon, they would regard them both as titans of industry, rather than the mere pawns he had often felt himself to be.

With each word, his spirits were soaring, the delight of power tickling the edges of his conscience.

The mayor, now hanging onto each syllable with ravenous intensity, stirred with underhanded delight; he too could see the promise in Blackthorn's proposition. There were nods of agreement, gestures of enthusiasm shared between men shaped by ambition, each reluctant to glance back upon their dubious morals and instead fixating upon the horizon beckoning them with promises of fortune.

For they, like the Scrooge of old, weighed up everything solely according to its gain.

Thus, in that moment, the genesis of a dark and ambitious camaraderie was forged.

Two souls bound together in a bond not of friendship, but of shared conquest, their eyes glistening with the unholy fire of greed that burned beneath their skins.

The stage was set, and they were but players, ready to enact a most fiendish drama cunningly concealed behind a façade of respectability and benevolence. A day of reckoning enthralled them.

Thus, with a gleam in his malicious eyes, Blackthorn reveled in delicious anticipation of the scheme unfolding in all its inglorious, devious, insolent and wicked splendor.

The wheel of fortune would spin, and he intended to be the one to steer it in directions better suited to his extremely greedy disposition, basking in the knowledge that he would soon become the architect of his own preposterous elevation, constructed upon the ruins of his competitor's intrinsic goodness.

The mayor, adjusting his spectacles with the air of a man perceiving himself sagacious in matters of governance, peered uneasily at Mr. Blackthorn, curiosity simmering beneath his portly exterior.

"Pray tell, Mr. Blackthorn," he inquired, his voice rich with condescension and feigned cordiality, "and what precisely do you propose we do with this street urchin— this lad of whom you speak, who has, as you say, wormed his way into the affections of Mr. Scrooge? Surely, you do not suggest we engage in some sordid charade, do you? For I must confess, while my ambitions are commendable, I find myself less inclined to theatrics that might cause a scandal most unseemly."

"Precisely! I'll tell you what we shall do. We will make full use of this Tom, this wayward and insipid lad who has squirmed his way into Scrooge's affections," Blackthorn replied, his voice filled with cunning and devious excitement, bound using strands of insidious glee.

He went on, "To the common eye, of course, he is naught but a charming street urchin deserving of much pity, but we shall paint him as a thieving rogue, a terrible scoundrel! Believe me, one deftly planted item within his satchel shall bring Scrooge's empire of benevolence to the brink of disgrace!

"With your own endorsement, we can ensure the bobbies are eager to lend a hand in this, the wickedest of endeavors. They could be persuaded, perhaps, that this young scamp is but a tool in Scrooge's devious machinations to build an army of delinquent wretches under his thumb!"

As he spoke, the room seemed to judder beneath his vision's bombastic audacity, its implications casting a cloud of possibility that enveloped the mayor, ensnaring his beleaguered conscience.

A sly smile crept across the mayor's lips.

It appeared he was contemplating the nefarious potential of the proposition laid before him.

"Ah! To twist the fickle nature of public sentiment to our advantage! It is genius, truly! You needn't worry about convincing the bobbies. Their hearsay and whims often favor those who line their pockets most generously. Furthermore," he declared, his tone threading through the air like a winding tale of deceit, "I shall ensure the Old Bailey's judge is suitably forewarned; he is forever receptive to my *in-duuuuucements;* I swear I can ride him like a rogue beast through all the alleys of London."

With each syllable of the crudely stretched word "inducements," he savored the delicious implied deceit, his voice rising and falling like the treble of an ominous melody, intoxicating in its promise of power. The notion of manipulating authority further exhilarated him, his phraseology dripping with an already present vision of scandalous triumph. Visions of vendetta simultaneously writhed, dancing before him like phantoms in the eternal twilight of his plotting mind.

"Indeed!" Blackthorn exclaimed, his heart swelling at the prospect of their scheme. "How wonderfully cruel it will be! Scrooge, who works so hard to elevate these children from the depths of despair, will be painted as the architect of unrest. The community will question his motives, cognizant not of his philanthropic heart but rather of a cunning ambition to seize what little power they desperately cling to! We will stoke the embers of discontent until they rage full into flame! Then, he will find himself sorely shunned."

"And the resulting discord," interjected the mayor, "shall render Scrooge's influence impotent, scattering both his coin and his reputation to all four winds. Let us not forget the power of word and rumor; they shall be our finest weapons. We have no need of a sword or poisonous substance since with each passing day, we will fan those flames until they are uncontrollable, his death knell!"

With this line of diabolical reasoning, the men firmly clasped hands, sealing the pact.

Thus, dark machinations spun on, a web of deceit laid over the innocent. London stood on the precipice of a dire confrontation between the serpent of industrial greed and the fragile blossoms of hope and promise blooming bravely in the hearts of its newly healthy, delighted children.

***

Mr. Blackthorn, a vile figure draped in shadow and cunning ambition, found himself at the threshold of the dingy jewelry factory, a place where the clatter of machines echoed like the relentless ticking of a clock. Each chime reminded the owner, Mr. Hargrove, of the debts tethering him to servitude.

The factory owner greeted him with a hollow smile, the kind one wears when being forced to dance with the devil. Mr. Hargrove was indeed beholden to Mr. Blackthorn, ensnared in a web of financial ruin and unfulfilled obligations, while the treasures of gold and gem crafted within those grimy walls gleamed mockingly in a dank and oppressive, seedy gloom.

"Ah, Hargrove, my dear friend," Blackthorn began, his voice dripping with the saccharine tones of false camaraderie, a *faux ami* indeed. "I trust your operations run smoothly? Or is it, perchance, that you find yourself once again teetering on the precipice of grave misfortune?"

Hargrove shifted uneasily, glancing at the floor as though it might offer him an escape from the unfortunate reality looming over him.

"I—I—I manage, Mr. Blackthorn; the times are tough as you know, but I, I get by. I—"

"Nonsense!" Blackthorn interrupted with a wave of his hand, a smile that barely reached his eyes transforming his visage into something grotesque. "It appears you are in need of further assistance—a little… *induuuuucement,* you might say. I can see it from here."

Blackthorn relished using the mayor's newly explained term, finding it carried a most pleasant tone to his ear. He leaned closer, the stench of ambition wafting off him. "You see, I have a most delightful plan requiring your cooperation. A charming young lad, a mere street urchin named Tom, has unwittingly become the apple of Mr. Scrooge's eye. Imagine the chaos! What if, by some fortuitous accident, a brooch—a trinket of exquisite value, perhaps—found its way into the boy's possession?"

Hargrove's brow furrowed as he digested the unseemly mix of words.

"You mean to frame him, sir?"

"Precisely!" Blackthorn exclaimed, diffusing the dark notion with a wave of his hand. "Think of it as an investment in your survival! An item, artfully planted on the boy—swiped from your factory, no doubt—will serve as the finest bait to ensnare Scrooge in the net of public disgrace. Do so, and your debts vanish like smoke in the wind, and I shall ensure you remain unharmed. After all, we must all play our parts to perfection in this grand performance, mustn't we?"

The factory owner paled as the enormity of Blackthorn's proposition struck home.

What choice had he, save to comply with the sinister machinations of a man who held his fate within his grasp? Blackthorn's lips curled into a satisfying smirk as he watched Hargrove, a once proud man, withering under the weight of corruption now clawing at his soul.

Hargrove offered a slow nod of agreement, his face a sudden canvas of resigned defeat.

Knowing he had ensnared Hargrove in his web, Mr. Blackthorn stepped from the factory, triumphant, convinced that victory was his for the taking.

And soon, he would have it!

***

In a patch of sunshine amidst the squalor of London's slumlands, there stood the office of Mr. Ebenezer Scrooge, a man who, but a decade prior, had cultivated a reputation as the personification of self-indulgence. Yet now, transformed by the spectral visitations that had stirred his heart from its wintry slumber, he was basking in the warm glow of purpose and goodwill. With the passing of the days, he found himself ever more besotted with generosity's virulence, moving among the citizens of London as a benevolent spirit, eager to cultivate kindness in hearts long hardened by want and neglect.

"Charity begets charity!" he would exclaim to astonished associates, urging them to see beyond their own toiling. "Why, my dear Bob Cratchit, you are a sure witness of the rippling effect of a single act of goodwill upon the lives of many. Why, even that miserable old hermit next door—who frowns as though he were born with a scowl—can be softened by a token of kindness!"

As Scrooge continued his self-appointed mission to mend the fabric of society, spreading the gospel of charitable living at every turn, he took great joy in witnessing positive changes in the faces of children and adults alike. A group of wide-eyed street urchins, whom he would often greet with a coin and a smile, seemed almost to reflect the light now searing within them.

Their laughter echoed through the streets, a sound so foreign to the once-grim atmosphere enveloping them. This small corner of the city might have been mistaken for another world entirely.

But little did Scrooge know that a storm was brewing just beyond the horizon, a malevolent scheme carefully orchestrated by Mr. Blackthorn and the hapless Mr. Hargrove, who was now entwined within his own web of fear and obligation. The factory owner, under the steely gaze of his manipulator, was laden with guilt, yet paralyzed by the prospect of ruin should he fail to execute the dastardly plot.

Meanwhile, back at the factory, the nefarious plan was set into motion.

Reddington, Hargrove's most trusted but morally bankrupt foreman, was instructed to pilfer a beautiful brooch from the display case meant for well-heeled patrons.

In the dim light of the evening, the foreman conducted his furtive affair, slipping the bauble into a small pocket with all the learned dexterity of a seasoned thief.

"Momentarily, we shall lay our trap," Blackthorn sneered, already chuckling.

He allied himself with Hargrove, the malignancy of his intentions barely concealed beneath a slimy veneer of charm. "No more delays, dear Hargrove. Your financial salvation lies in framing that boy! In the coming days, while Scrooge parades his fanciful delusions of grandeur, the good people will witness his downfall thanks to little Tom. His anguish shall serve your interests, and in the blissful aftermath, you will walk free! A desperate man's salvation always necessitates another's demise."

***

Scrooge, blissfully oblivious to the treacheries unfolding, was preoccupied with devising a surprise feast for the Cratchit family.

He envisioned a bountiful table laden with turkey, pudding, and a flurry of laughter.

"I will light their humble abode as though it were a palace!" he uttered with a gleeful chuckle, rubbing his hands in anticipation. "Now, where did I put those invitations? Yes, yes! A merry gathering—just what they deserve! It will be the best ever end to their year!"

On a crisp afternoon, the sun nestling stubbornly behind the clouds, Mr. Scrooge—now a man smitten with merriment—ventured into the bustling marketplace, his heart buoyed by uncommon jubilation. He strode through throngs of vendors, their shouts ringing in harmonic disarray, a chorus of joyful spirits long quelled beneath the oppressive weight of duty and despair.

With each step, he bore not the heavy chains of avarice but rather an eagerness to procure a veritable feast for the Cratchits, those dear souls whose laughter had, in a few short months, become a call for goodwill within his habitually taciturn heart. Today, his soul was already making merry at the promise of such an innocent pleasure, the delight he could give to others who did deserve it so.

"So, then, what shall it be?" he contemplated, eyes aglow as he perused the verdant stalls, ablaze with an abundance of fresh produce, glistening meats, and sweet sugared confections. "A turkey, fat and plump! A pudding, rich and fragrant! And I must remember to put fine, shiny shillings into it … And perhaps—oh, yes!— the finest claret for a toast to those who know the truest warmth of family!"

With each selection, he delighted in the exchange with the jovial vendors, whose eyes brightened at his exemplary generosity. In that bustling bazaar, framed by the fading glow of winter's sun, Ebenezer Scrooge served as a veritable Father Christmas of the marketplace. He sparkled with delights gentle and profound as the spirit of giving skittered about him like a familiar presence, whispering words of joy and festivity.

***

On a crisp and frosty morning, the cheerful sight of holly wreaths adorning windows and the promise of goodwill daring to warm winter's grasp, Mr. Hargrove, the beleaguered factory owner, donned his finest coat. It was frayed at the cuffs, borrowed from a far more prosperous time.

With his breaths clouding the air before him, he strode purposefully toward the market square, where vendors were already calling to passersby with voices as lively as their wares.

A cacophony of hawkers was also weaving through the throngs of townsfolk.

There, among the stalls bursting with vibrant produce and sweet treats, he spied Mr. Ebenezer Scrooge. Once synonymous with meanness, he had reinvented himself.

Now, no one could deny he had turned into an unexpectedly generous gentleman.

Approaching with purposeful intent, a curious dread surged within Hargrove, mingling with a dash of hope momentarily quelling the tempest of desperation brewing in his soul.

After all, the spirit of Mr. Scrooge had undergone a miraculous metamorphosis; it would take a deft hand to manipulate such kindness, he mused, foreboding whispering caution into his ear.

"If the winds of fortune shall favor me today, then let us see how this genteel spirit can be swayed!" So spoke Scrooge, with a hearty cheer quite foreign to his former self.

"Ah, Scrooge!" Hargrove exclaimed, feigning undue surprise as he stepped into the fray of merchants and customers. "What a splendid opportunity to cross paths in such delightful surroundings! A chance to exchange pleasantries amidst the hustle and bustle of the market, would you not agree?"

"Mr. Hargrove! Indeed, a fine day, is it not?" Scrooge replied, his visage buoyed with an unnatural lightness. "You find me on a quest for provisions for this evening's feast. Are you prepared to partake in my humble efforts to bring cheer to the Cratchit family? A fine group of spirits they are, deserving of all good things money can acquire."

"Why, sir, you continue to astonish me with your boundless charity!" Hargrove replied.

His voice was syrupy, a honeyed balm masking all the treachery bubbling beneath.

"Indeed, it is by such noble endeavors that I am gladdened to find you here. Might I implore you, in the spirit of camaraderie, to consider a partnership, one that could intertwine our fates for the good of the laboring common folks of the city?"

Scrooge leaned in, enraptured by Hargrove's effusive proposition. It was most unexpected.

"Partnership, you say? Why, a splendid notion! Together, we might cultivate a venture most worthwhile, supporting those in need and fostering a society in which every man helps every other man! Sir, I could hardly think of a more gratifying endeavor! Splendid, splendid."

And there, amidst the enticing aromas and vibrant colors of the market, Mr. Hargrove smiled.

It was a smile edged with iron, a mask he wore with increasing deftness as he spun his stealthy web of ill-intentioned deceit. "Certainly, sir! With your wisdom guiding our endeavors, we shall unleash a wave of improvement for the many! Let us recount the good we intend to accomplish hand in hand. With your prowess, we can change lives! Let no man try to stand in our way!"

"Yes, my generous friend! You must join us in our meetings intended to lift the poor out of poverty."

Scrooge beamed, unaware that each jovial phrase was one step further toward sealing his fate with an invisible thread, tethering him to a duplicitous soul as the wraith of betrayal loomed ever closer.

While Mr. Scrooge remained blissfully ignorant of the carefully crafted artifice laid before him, the insidious designs of Blackthorn were lurking, churning in the shadows, waiting patiently for the moment when the fabric of trust would unravel, leaving nothing but ruin in its wake.

And as the marketplace chattered with incessant life, one wondered how long the buoyancy of hope might endure against the inevitable tide of calamity soon to wash upon their shores.

As night descended across London, Blackthorn's sinister plot came together, and the trap soon lay ready to ensnare the unsuspecting Scrooge.

The joy filling his heart and soul was not merely borne of personal triumphs.

It demonstrated in all its glory his metamorphosis, yet at the same time, the embodiment of wickedness was advancing swiftly but surely toward a reckoning he could scarcely imagine.

Chapter 9: A New Christmas Spirit

The air of London carried winter's cruel bite, crisp as the freshly fallen frost adorning all the windowpanes. Yet within the entangled streets, a fretful tension was soon to be unleashed, threatening to unravel the happiness that Ebenezer Scrooge had been cultivating amidst this ebullient season.

As the days dwindled and the festive spirit came creeping into the hearts of the townsfolk, the air grew crisp with anticipation, decorated with the warm glow of hearths alight.

The season of giving was again approaching, the promise of Christmas Day twinkling like a star in the evening sky, casting joyful luminescence upon all who wandered the streets.

Christmas' pinnacle was mere days away.

Already, the atmosphere was electric, alive with laughter ringing through the frosty twilight.

The scent of roasted chestnuts and spiced cider wafted invitingly through the air, heralding the arrival of the most beloved holiday of the year.

In this atmosphere of goodwill and charity, Mr. Ebenezer Scrooge was lovingly preparing to host his very special gathering, into which he had poured his passion and his heart for so long now.

Among the guests, Mr. Hargrove found himself seated at Scrooge's sprawling banquet table, bedecked with a bounty worthy of a king.

Yet, even amidst the jovial clatter of plates and the many gleeful toasts raised to the spirit of the season, a subtle tremor was coursing through his veins, a sinister confoundment festering.

As he absorbed the rapturous delight of fellow revelers, the merriment felt like a gilded cage, each chuckle adding to the turmoil roiling within his despondent heart.

What is this wretched turmoil? He pondered the question as the twinkling lights cast their whimsical glow upon the festive fare. It was not remorse, for he had long ago buried that emotion beneath layers of ambition; rather, it was a prickling unease, a creeping tendril of doubt at the back of his mind—a reminder that deceit, once set in motion, seldom danced unaccompanied.

Hargrove's thoughts turned to young Tom, with his innocent charm and bright-eyed hope. How could he, an agent of reluctant calamity, dare weave a shadow so dark around a young soul so pure?

Yet, he felt the weight of opportunity pressing hard on his conscience as he prepared to deliver the tiny, glinting brooch into the depths of Tom's bag.

A nervous anticipation twisted in his gut and refused to be quelled.

He had fashioned this scheme with all the meticulous precision of a master artisan, but now, at the threshold of his ill design, it felt more like a plunge into icy waters, uncertain and treacherous, a leap from which he may never return unscathed. The prospect of its execution was looming, bringing an uncanny dread haunting the edges of his thoughts. He understood all too well that nothing extinguished the holiday spirit quite as fiercely as the scent of betrayal. In that precarious moment, as he contemplated the depths of his impending deceit, his heart began quaking. It seemed on the verge of bursting forth from his ribcage, a captive bird desperate to escape a set of iron bars of its own making.

Was he really about to embark on this appalling task? Was there not time to—

"Pray, join us!" Scrooge declared as if from nowhere, his voice ringing with now customary joy as he welcomed his assembly of friends and strangers.

A motley crew they were, stiffened shirts and neat waistcoats mingling with frocks of lively colors, while children laughed and scampered about, their delight setting a vibrant, jovial tone.

Though the warmth enveloped Hargrove, a chill had settled itself deep in the pit of his stomach.

In truth, he feared that Scrooge might somehow be capable of discerning his true intentions.

With each toast raised and every hearty laugh shared, Mr. Hargrove observed Scrooge—the man who had metamorphosed into the embodiment of everything for which this season stood.

Benevolence, kindness, cheer and goodwill …

Christmas was for making amends, for welcoming old partnerships and friends, for drinking a toast to all things good in society, for creating new friendships, and for blessing the under-privileged.

But tonight was not merely a celebration; it was going to be a stage for Hargrove's grand design.

In the days preceding that moment, his devious plot had taken root, one that would entwine him ever more deeply in the fabric of Scrooge's rising esteem.

As for young Tom, the personification of innocence, was he also going to fall for the ruse? Unwittingly, he was devastatingly careening into the folds of Hargrove's treacherous scheme.

"Ah, yes—where is our dear young Tom?" Scrooge raised his glass, blissfully ignorant of the deception lurking behind Hargrove's charming façade. "He deserves a toast for all of his hard work!"

In that very moment cast against the backdrop of gaiety and light, Hargrove spied Tom in the throes of conversation, his young face glowing with unfiltered joy.

Caught in the tide of laughter, Tom appeared blissfully unwary of his surroundings as he set down his satchel, unguarded and oblivious to the footsteps of misfortune snapping at his heels.

With the nimbleness of a fox, Hargrove sauntered nonchalantly toward the unattended satchel, a cunning smile cloaked in the guise of delight. Within moments, his fingers deftly retrieved the coveted brooch—a precious bauble of considerable value, awaiting the hands of a noble lady yet to claim it—its gleam matching the malice mirrored in his eyes. Exactly as in his evil plan, he placed it carefully within the folds of Tom's satchel, ensuring this clandestine act of treachery would not be discovered until he had so artfully orchestrated the unfolding drama that would serve his interests.

"A most splendid gathering, indeed!" Hargrove crooned to those surrounding, moving seamlessly back to his seat. The filched artifact lay secure, now a hidden harbinger of his sinister intent.

As laughter crescendoed, Scrooge took to the center of the table, rallying his guests to consider the plights of others, a noble exhortation. Yet, as he was speaking of all great charitable ventures, Hargrove's secret was quietly nibbling away at the edges of the master goldsmith's conscience.

For while Scrooge may well have been the alchemist of all good in that moment, Hargrove had taken it upon himself to be the architect of discord, laying the groundwork for a colossal act of misery.

"Let us commit ourselves to the upliftment of others!" Scrooge boomed, unaware of the deceitful undertow ebbing just beneath the surface of these seemingly harmonious waters. "We shall be stewards of generosity and giving! Let no man, woman or child suffer or be alone and let no one starve!"

"Indeed, Mr. Scrooge!" Hargrove chimed in, attempting to deflect the gaze of suspicion, to avert the accusing eyes of those who might pierce the veil of his deceit. A viper coiled within his breast, its venomous fangs poised to strike should his treachery be uncovered. He raised his glass, though a harshness was lingering in the depths of his tone, a dissonance that would, in due time, reveal itself.

"May we all strive to heed your call, and together pave the way for an enlightened, kinder world!"

And so, as the evening wore on, it was but a matter of time before innocence would meet its ruin, the spirit of betrayal rising to shatter the fragile shell of acceptance so joyously enveloping everyone.

The balmy air had been stirred with unmet promises, yet at the same time, in hidden corners, malevolent shadows lurked, ready to coalesce into calamity.

Just as the air was curdling with Hargrove's torment, a resounding bang reverberated through the hall, a sharp, insistent sound that cleaved through the revelry like a knife through a rich plum pudding.

The grand doors swung open with a creak far more ominous than a funeral dirge, and in strode two grim-faced officers of the law, their uniforms crisp and their visages austere.

The fine wool of their dark blue frock coats spoke of unquestionable authority, commanding instant silence. Tall and broad-shouldered, they stood rigidly, white cotton gloves crisp and hands poised, suggesting both readiness and restraint. Stalwart helmets adorned their heads, slightly tipped forward over stern brows, while the faint scent of brimstone hinted at their steadfast vigilance.

This imposing presence was in contrast to the mirthful tableau, laughter in the grand hall faltering.

"Ladies and gentlemen," called one of the bobbies, "we regret to intrude upon this festive gathering, but we bring news of the utmost importance. Sadly, evidence has emerged that a brooch of tremendous value, recently purloined from the factory, lies concealed among this evening's guests."

Gasps punctuated the room, filling the air with palpable tension.

Mr. Hargrove felt a chill sweeping over him, as though winter's draught had intruded upon the warmth of the feast. He nearly recoiled as the gaze of the constable flitted over the assembled company, all shifting uneasily in their seats. The merry chatter had been replaced by a clamor of whispers, rippling through the crowd as a wave of panic. Hargrove, feeling as if the noose of suspicion was tightening second by second around his throat, fought to maintain an outward veneer of nonchalance.

"Pray, remain calm!" called the second officer, his brow furrowed. "We seek merely to ask a few questions and, if need be, conduct a search for the good of all present. No one need fear unless they have something unseemly to hide."

There followed an uneasy shifting of chairs as guests exchanged furtive glances. Hargrove's heart raced anew, a tempest of dread threatening to spill over. In that moment, he understood the precarious balance of his malefactions teetering on the precipice of exposure. This did not feel good anymore.

He was to be the key witness in this farcical framing of an innocent young lad, all on behalf of Mr. Blackthorn and those wishing to see the demise of this do-gooder, Ebenezer Scrooge.

Indeed, once or twice, he almost got to his feet, wanting to cry out, "The boy is innocent!"

As Tom, blissfully unaware, scooted to the seat's edge, clutching tightly his glass of punch as if it were some form of lifeline, another wave of guilt crashed over the jittery Hargrove.

This appalling, thoughtless act was threatening to drown him in a maelstrom of remorse he'd considered himself well beyond. What was to become of him?

Would not all the weight of his wretched sin—his artful deception—become unmasked this night, amidst the sparkle of the chandelier and the merry mirth he had also plotted to purloin?

The tension in the room reached a boiling point as the constables, unsatisfied after their queries, began their search, methodically sifting through the elegant weaves of ostentation adorning the manor.

Cries of alarm and astonishment erupted among the guests, as if a thunderstorm had swept through.

The clink of silverware and the rustle of embroidered fine silken attire gave way to hushed tones.

With a curiosity both dreadful and compulsive, Hargrove watched as one officer approached young Tom; the young boy's eyes gleamed with true innocence, the mirthful glint of a soul untouched by wealth or guilt. Guilelessly unaware of the tempest brewing just beyond the periphery of his youthful exuberance, he had come to this gathering as a mere guest, a humble learner in a grand, bold scheme.

"Now, what have we here?" the constable exclaimed, stooping to examine Tom's modest satchel gifted to him by Scrooge himself, its worn leather indicative of many a road traveled.

The assemblage fell into a hush, all eyes scanning the officer's hands as if they were magic-wielding sorcerers casting a spell on this blemish-free and unsuspecting lad.

With one swift movement, the constable raised the bag, and there, nestled amidst humble garments and well-used books, lay the brooch, its lustrous gems blinding onlookers when it caught the light.

A loud gasp of accusation hurled the jollity of the evening into a deep, shocked sadness.

The startled gazes and discourse ensuing were a lamentation, each guest drowning in disbelief.

"Officer, I didn't take it! I swear it!" Tom stammered, his voice trembling as confusion and fear dawned. "Sir, I never saw it before!" He looked so small, so deathly afraid.

But in his face was more than that; above all, he looked confused, bewildered, and innocent.

Hargrove felt his heart lurch, knowing that within the depths of that innocent boy's spirit lay the only truth of the matter. Yet rampant suspicion was a wild beast not easily tamed, and even the gentlest of souls could find themselves ensnared in its merciless grip by accident or ill will.

But justice, the kind blinded to circumstance and cloaked in the law's inflexible decorum, had spoken, making its feeling known. The officer, resolute in his duty, gripped young Tom by the arm, imprisoning him in the cruel grasp of Darby handcuffs made of iron and linked by a weighty chain.

Roughly, he led him away from the gathering with a firm and callous grasp.

In his hardened certainty, he offered no solace to the boy, dismissing his silent dread as though the child's fate were already written and the world's cruelties far beyond question.

"Don't fret, lad! If you are truly innocent, we will see the truth come to light!" came the constable's voice, a wry smile pursing the corners of his lips.

The words fell upon deaf ears, poor Tom's anguished gaze flitting about wildly, seeking the support of his fellow guests; he found only a sea of downcast faces bearing expressions of concern mingled with suspicion, each one retreating inward, unwilling to confront this manifest, abject darkness.

It was a precarious situation indeed, and no one wanted anything to do with this awful affair.

Meanwhile, old Ebenezer Scrooge was lingering there at the back of the throng, his countenance shadowed by a pall of melancholy. He had come here expecting a carefully planned evening of merriment, the gaiety of song and laughter, the bright faces of friends and family rekindling the spirit of the season long shut away. He had expected drinking and dancing, many a jig in celebration of the season and the good things to come for all who did godly work.

Yet as the unfolding drama played out, he felt as if all the phantoms of his own past had crept forth from the cobwebbed corners of his memory, whispering tales of folly, reminding him of the long-lasting scourge of wealth won through questionable means.

Is justice always so swift to condemn, yet so slow to discern? he pondered silently, his thoughts churning as the officer led a tearful, protesting Tom away.

The boy's sore complaints rang out loudly through the cavernous silence left in his wake.

As for Scrooge, he was bereft. This was all of his doing, it had to be. The boy was blameless!

"Tom, you're innocent! This isn't the end for you," Scrooge called as the hapless lad was led away, chains clinking, the elder benefactor's plaintive voice rising above the hushed murmurs of the crowd.

"Do not lose hope! The truth will out! Justice will prevail; there are those who see beyond the surface. Something questionable has been done to you this night; I will uncover it, mark my words!"

Hargrove almost leaped from his shaking, sweaty skin.

Chapter 10: A Trial of Innocence

The next day—its morning sun struggling to break the gloom of cloud and suspicion—found Ebenezer Scrooge draped in a tattered overcoat.

He appeared cowed, defeated, beset by untold worries and lies.

Trudging through murky streets, he was heading toward the imposing edifice of the local gaol.

As he approached, his mind heaved with thoughts of poor unsuspecting Tom, caught in a snare laid by malice and quarrels, and no doubt delivered by some hopeless, arrogant, embittered industrialist.

Upon entering the gaol, the atmosphere stung with the acrid scent of tears and stagnant air, pulled down by the many regrets of the incarcerated and accused. A stout figure in uniform, stoic and imposing, stood guard at the entrance, glancing over Scrooge with an aura of suspicion suggesting he had set eyes on far too many faces belonging to greedy souls intent only on sneaky deception.

"What brings you here, sir?" the gaoler barked, a suspicious glint in his eye as if he surmised Scrooge's heart was an unfathomable well of guile.

"I am here," Scrooge replied, his voice a guarded tremor born of unfamiliar resolve, "to speak with Tom. The lad deserves counsel, and I intend to offer it to the boy."

With a grunt of acknowledgment, the gaoler led him deep into the dank corridors, iron bars clanging shut behind them. As he took each reluctant step, Scrooge's mind could only consider the weight of the world pressing against those fragile bars, particularly the innocence of a boy whose misfortune had sprouted from the evening's folly and beyond that, from Scrooge's well-intended eve.

"Here, I bring you to Treacherous Thomas!" the officer shouted as he arrived at a dimly lit cell, the bars creating intimidating shadows, stick-thin specters sliding across a slabbed cold stone floor.

Tom looked up, his visage marred by worry in the dimness of the tiny cell. The boy was not even jailed alone; Scrooge had not even considered the dangers of this godforsaken place—how cramped it might be, how the boy would find himself among murderers and poisoners, how he would be bullied and ridiculed, and so much worse in this, the most hopeless and hideous of institutions.

Here came men who had slit the throats of wives and travelers, men who had boiled babes alive on their own stoves at midnight to save pennies by no longer needing to feed them.

Here came men who had committed acts of treason of the gravest kind.

And here came, apparently, little boys with pale faces and baggy pants, begging to be understood and heard and believed. Upon seeing Scrooge, anticipation and glee lit the young lad's troubled face, though it was tempered by an underlying fear that persisted in clinging on.

He looked so lost, so desperate, so frightened.

"Mr. Scrooge," Tom murmured, his voice quivering as if grappling with disbelief that this formidable figure would come to visit him in such a grim sanctuary, comprehending his difficulty.

"Tom," Scrooge interrupted, his words steeling with fresh conviction. He placed both hands on the crudely cast-iron bars as if wishing he had the strength to bend them and free the poor boy then and there. "I stand before you this day not as your mentor, but as a man who has witnessed a grievous wrong, one I fully intend to right. You must know, lad, that I swear to do all within my power to prove your innocence, for it is evident that fate has conspired against you in a manner most cruel and unjust.

"Or perhaps it was not fate that conspired if you get my drift, Tom. Perhaps it was man himself. I fear you have been the unwitting victim of a plot as wicked as any that ever reached my ears."

"But the brooch was found in my bag!" Tom protested, his eyes showing a youthful, desperate sincerity. "What hope is there? How can I prove myself against accusations of a theft so visible?"

"Hope is a fragile thing, young man," Scrooge replied, his countenance softening in a manner previously alien to him before his transformation. "But it must not be extinguished. Was it not you who demonstrated kindness to your fellow students of life with unwavering spirit? We shall summon that same spirit now, and united, we will seek the way to the truth. I know it can be done."

"Mr. Scrooge," Tom said hesitantly. "I—I am grateful, but the evidence … it seems insurmountable, sir, a tidal wave flung in my direction. And I am but one man, an innocent, no less! But how can I prove it? I'm up for transportation, sir. They mean to send me to the penal colonies of Australia!"

Tom flinched, his young frame trembling.

He was suddenly overcome by the grim notion of exile to that distant, merciless destination, where the unyielding soil and the company of hardened malefactors promised only mistreatment and lies.

Concealing the tremor of dread creeping through his heart as he dwelt upon the foreboding prospect of this virtuous boy's lot in a far-off penal colony, Scrooge summoned what little mental strength he could muster, using it to fashion a few words of hollow encouragement.

"Evidence, my dear boy, can be a fickle mistress! Often, it is shrouded in shadows only able to be illuminated by the persistence of the righteous. We must survey the ground from whence that brooch came, revisit the evening's revelry, and examine the character of all present. Therein lies your certain salvation! Boy, I say to you again, have faith. If not faith in yourself, if not in this miserable circumstance, then please find a way to have faith in me. Believe that I will not forsake you."

The determination in Scrooge's voice rattled Tom to his core.

He leaned against the bars of his cell, hope rekindling in his chest, and all at once, the horrors of imprisonment felt a touch lighter.

"You—the kindest soul I ever did meet, sir. Truly, would you do so? You would fight for me?"

"I would and I will, with all that I am," Scrooge declared, his fingers gripping the bars, so desperate to have the barrier removed so that he could hug the boy. "I promise you, you will walk free."

Tom had just said that he was but one man, an innocent man.

If only Scrooge could see it himself! Truth was, he saw before him no man at all, only a scared, unwitting child on the cusp of his journey to maturity. What a poor beginning this was, all due to someone's unforgiveable, inconceivably ugly machinations.

Determined, Scrooge hurriedly made his way toward his home that had played host to merriment on the night of the theft. He would not rest until he had unearthed the truth, for in the pursuit of justice stood the opportunity to reforge bonds, to restore integrity to a family so unjustly threatened.

Perhaps he could really liberate another heart, not only the one shackled by metal.

It was strange indeed, but compassion had reanimated within his weary soul, burdened by the pervasive state of greed, ignorance, and want in the world.

Perhaps he could also free whichever villain had committed this act, bringing him to goodness.

It was what he hoped for. He vowed to free Tom, to clear his name, to see him do well for himself in the world, and he wished to see Tom released from viewing the world as such an unkind place.

But beyond that, he wanted to see the perpetrator regretful, willing and begging to reform.

***

The trial arrived just a day before Christmas—Christmas Eve morning to be precise, cloaked in a pall that matched the dismal foreboding of the Old Bailey courtroom itself.

Within the confines of the gaol where all things ruthless and unhappy reigned, Tom was waiting.

Scrooge sharpened his resolve as he made his way to the infamous court, a grand room that had lately borne witness to countless fates, some even worse than Tom's, some far less so.

Alas, Scrooge had hoped for the boy to receive his trial in the local assizes of a near county, hopeful for leniency for one with so unblemished a record and a purported first offense. Instead, deemed a citizen of London Town, the Old Bailey was to host his appearance. No one escaped lightly when a trial proceeded there, and on no occasion could man or boy speak in his own favor.

Less than a month ago, a woman had been sent to the colonies for stealing a slice of bread; justice had seen fit to part from her children who would be sent to the workhouse. She was deemed most fortunate when one of the children shortly came of age, removing them all to the same penal colony.

Around the same time, a child had been committed to a year's incarceration and a public shaming for hiding himself within a public house after nightfall, all with the aim to take gin.

It was not because of his predilection to drink.

No, it was to sanitize his ailing mother's ulcerated leg.

Still, no one found mercy for him either.

And a grown man had been sentenced to a whipping for the most minor of property crimes, the inadvertent burning down of a neighbor's chicken coop while trying to warm himself, finding himself locked outside on a merciless winter's night. He had paid handsomely in coin for the reparations, yet still, he had been made a scapegoat, paraded through the streets like wickedness itself.

Outside the weathered stone building, a palpable sense of dread seized the hearts of those gathered. Friends of Tom and passersby alike had crowded there, hunched in their overcoats and standing for many hours, each one acutely aware that the outcome of this trial carried an impact for everyone.

A great rift had emerged among the populace, cleaving the city into two factions.

On one side were those steadfastly proclaiming Tom's innocence, convinced that a lad of his tender years and evident good, clean record could not be guilty of so grave a crime.

And for what, moreover? Why would he do such a thing when already sheltered under the care of one as benevolent as Mr. Scrooge? The lad already had a path to learning, a roof, and a steady job.

Led by Scrooge, the faction in favor of the boy muttered darkly of a conspiracy, of an innocent boy ensnared by the machinations of grown men far more corrupt than he could ever be.

Yet, across the cobbled streets and crowded taverns, another narrative was gaining swift traction, seeded and nurtured by the mayor and his allies within the city's closed industrial associations.

Through their iron grip upon the presses, they unleashed a torrent of broadsheets, pamphlets, and notices, each one dripping with insinuation and direct accusation. These proclamations painted Tom and Scrooge as a pair of cunning deceivers, their purported acts of charity being but a velvet glove masking an iron fist, clutching at power and wealth with merciless greed.

This tale, spun with such artful malice, swept through the city like a plague, carried lip to lip until even those with no cause to care found themselves entangled in the unseemly discord.

London had become a crucible of rumor and division, its citizens united only in the uneasy certainty that the forthcoming trial would leave no one untouched.

The judge sat with the clout of authority on his broad shoulders, an unyielding figure, imposing in a long wig and dark gown, his face somberly dressed in a perpetual scowl to which its many flabby folds seemed to bear witness. He bore the name of Justice, yet his eyes reflected pure greed.

Judge Wilkins, a man of stout demeanor and gloriously luxuriant whiskers, was known to be in collusion with the Mayor of London and the industrialist elite, particularly with Mr. Blackthorn, a figure with fingers steeped deep in the underbelly of commerce and the dirty secrets of affluence.

True to his sinister promise, the mayor, with a cunning hand and a heart blackened by ambition, had contrived to set the wheels in motion, ensuring that Tom would be denied the justice of a jury trial.

Instead, the young man's fate had been cast into the clutches of this one man, a single corrupt judge.

The room bore a somber silence as Scrooge took his place, a lone sentinel on a fortress of moral rectitude. Young Tom was almost dragged into the dock; he was not even putting up a fight, yet the gaolers saw fit to make every step more arduous, to cause a scuffle such that any onlooker would receive the spectacle for which they had undoubtedly come along. They pulled him along, knowing the boy, whose legs were fastened with cuffs and a hefty chain, could not possibly move any faster.

Yet more pale and drawn than the last time on which Scrooge had set eyes on him, it was as if all lifeblood had been siphoned from him by the hands of harsh fate or the secret tortures of cellmates.

Scrooge's heart was bleeding, aching for the innocent boy, entangled as he was in a web spun by those who wielded influence with a capriciousness wholly unfitting of their power and status.

Whispers from haughty spectators ricocheted off the walls of the grand spectacle, a veritable amphitheater of human curiosity and folly, with its high arched windows filtering in narrow shafts of dim light, drawing attention to the minuscule dust motes flitting through the musty air.

The walls, adorned with somber mahogany panels, loomed like grim sentinels of justice, while rows of peculiar onlookers, straining upon their benches, leaned nearly out of their seats. They were anxious to partake in the morbid drama unfolding before them, having indeed come to revel in a show.

Above it all, an ornately decorated plaster ceiling bore witness to the proceedings, adorned with allegorical paintings of Justice holding her scales, ever-balanced yet all too often treated with the petulance of a child clasping tight to a toy. The tall, imposing pillars framing the room seemed to resonate with the weight of centuries of jurisprudence, the ideals of mercy and punishment being routinely debated in earnest, yet oftentimes meeting with the menace of hypocrisy.

"Order!" barked the judge. "We stand here today in pursuit of truth, though I shall remind you that truth can oft be a fleeting vision when the darkness of man's deceit encroaches!"

As the formalities commenced, Scrooge steeled himself.

As he saw it, he bore full responsibility.

His position was the only defense against this tide of well-heeled corruption threatening to also swallow up an innocent lad. Scrooge's mind, once clouded by his own past greed, was now clear, bustling with determination to wrestle justice from the maw of those who had fashioned this travesty.

Mr. Blackthorn looked more corpulent than ever, swathed in unjust finery masking the festering corruption of his soul; he lounged smugly in the gallery, all former nerves set aside, his cold, calculating eyes appraising the proceedings with the rapacity of a wolf stalking its helpless prey.

The witnesses, their tongues steeped in deceit and their palms plentifully greased with ill-gotten coin, began the weft of their damning tales.

One by one, they spun a sinister picture in which they cast young Tom not merely as a desperate thief but also as a cunning accomplice to none other than Ebenezer Scrooge, that wily conman.

"Ebenezer Scrooge has been using the boy as a pawn in his dirty game of power!" they asserted. "Beneath the veneer of respectability, this man schemes and plots to bend the city to his will and rule it as an unchallenged despot. The brooch is but a solitary trifling token in a web of calculated villainy—a leaf upon the dark and turbulent tide of a chronicled wickedness!"

These 'witnesses' were drowning poor Tom in the merciless, biased court of public opinion.

Suddenly, overcome by a surge of raw emotion and a burning desire to save his dear Tom, Scrooge rose unbidden, voice crackling but fierce. "It's not true!" Scrooge interjected out of turn, not for a moment taking on board how his outburst may be perceived; indeed, he and the boy were supposed to stay silent, but how could Scrooge do that? He was determined to be heard, otherwise, how would anyone understand Tom's innocence?

Scrooge fired back in a tone most plaintive, "I beseech you, allow the truth out, if but for a moment! Raise the curtain of deception that cloaks this ... travesty of justice! They have framed the boy!"

"Your begging is unwelcome and futile!" the judge snapped, glaring as if Scrooge were an impudent scamp, snaring attention with unwarranted bravado. "You will not divert the court with your theatrics, or it will be deemed perjury of the utmost order! Proceed with the evidence!"

Reluctantly, Scrooge acquiesced, though defiance had ignited in his core.

As the proceedings continued, testimonies twined around Tom like creeping vines, weaving an inescapable noose about his scrawny neck. Scrooge's mood sank to hear the poignant declaration of a so-called witness, a shifty-eyed fellow in a shabby, many-holed coat.

The liar's face oozed troubles earned through liquor and ill, greatly misjudged company.

"I saw him!" the man claimed, his voice rising in a tone grating with accusation. "The lad was lurking near the display case where the jewels were displayed. Quick as a rat, and thrice as slippery! A thief, I tell you, a thief! He took the brooch from its safe place as surely as I stand here. The boy deserves a good whipping! Aye, he is a blot upon the purity and honesty of men like our complainant."

Scrooge's mind raced, justice and righteousness slipping from his grasp.

He could already hear the glum pronouncement due to seal Tom's fate.

The judge, brimming and puffing himself up with self-satisfaction, even seemed to savor the impending condemnation; after all, ensuring the profits of Mr. Blackthorn's industrial empire required tightly-woven cords of judicial compliance. But Ebenezer Scrooge would not stand for it!

He was not yet done, rising again to his feet, his face mottled with the ailing discoloration of a man whose blood looked set to burst through his eyes.

"It's preposterous, this … tissue of impudent lies!" he spat, undeterred by the previous threat of punishment. "You, sir, are supposed to be a judge, a man of God swearing on the good book, the Bible, a man who speaks before the Lord in favor of all that is faithful and true! Surely, there is more to this than hearsay! Context is truth's handmaiden!"

He was reduced to desperation, leveling a fierce glare at the judge.

"Tom, tell them!" he added in a wailing shriek. "Tell them they set you up!"

The wretched boy uttered not a peep, remaining head down, seemingly staring at the polished top of the table before him. His face showed that he already accepted his fate, the ready condemnation certain to pursue him. Little did Scrooge know that Tom had been threatened by the gaolers that they would kill Scrooge if he spoke in his own defense as an added deterrent despite knowing he would never be permitted to speak in the rigged court.

Momentarily, his pained eyes looked up, weeping, his small body a-tremble, and his gaze seeming to say in silence, *but there is no point, Mr. Scrooge. Nobody believes me innocent, and I will not put my benefactor in jeopardy, even if it means my own life is ruined.*

"Enough!" declared the judge standing tall, pulling on his robes in a gesture of status and insistence.

He waving an imperious hand, dismissing Scrooge with the flick of his wrist as though he were but a bothersome fly. "The evidence is incontrovertible, and no alibi will save a confirmed scoundrel from facing the consequences of his misdeeds. One more utterance from you in defiance of the procedures of this court of law, and I shall have you—"

He had no opportunity to finish.

Again breaking all decorum and formality of the day, Scrooge's howls of defiance would not relent, rudely cutting through the judge's words, inviting. "Arrest me, then! Take me, take me instead of the boy! Take me to prison, have me whipped, chain me and flog me. I truly do not care one jot! And why do I not care?"

Two constables grabbed him beneath both arms, ready to drag him away.

"Have him for perjury!" a man shouted from the gallery.

The judge wiped his sweaty head with the back of his hand, then delved into a drawer for his red-spotted silk handkerchief. He wiped his nose, all while Scrooge continued shouting, "That's right, do your worst to me! Because the boy is good, the boy is an innocent, and the boy's case deserves to be heard! I am not afraid of the likes of you. You cannot condemn an innocent soul without pausing to consider the tides of corruption lapping at your shores! I implore you, gentlemen, to question the fabric of this charge. And should you refuse to take statements for the accused, then hang me in his stead."

At last, a chilling apprehension settled upon Scrooge, revealing the audacious folly of his impulsive outburst. He had, with a single, unauthorized utterance, struck at the very foundations of that ancient, unyielding legal system, disturbing its formal dictates and the precise order of its advocates. Yet, though the true peril of his breach now rushed upon him like an icy tide, his heart, newly emboldened, held firm in its desperate plea for justice.

The judge's brows rose, as if for a moment he was considering how any man could offer his own life on the line unless he truly believed in another's innocence. He said nothing.

"Will you not have us take him?" one of the constables asked, tired of wrestling this miscreant into some semblance of compliance. The other officer grappled to keep Scrooge's arm in his grasp.

"I … I will think on it," proclaimed the judge, gesturing for the court to be seated again, and calm.

Yet as the trial continued in its grimness, Scrooge's pleas against the shambling revelations seemed to fade into the ether of the court, mere murmurings devoured by the grandiosity of falsehood.

There was little hope left for Tom.

The breath caught in Scrooge's throat, this expectant perfidious verdict looming large, ready to reverberate through the courtroom.

The judge, his face set like stone and his body bloated with puffery, declared loudly, "Quiet in my courtroom! I have heard enough! I am prepared to deliver my verdict."

Fixing his gaze on the boy, he commanded, "Thomas, rise and face the judgment of this court!"

The room fell into a hushed expectancy.

Tom, trembling throughout his weak body, stood before the imposing man's piercing stare.

"In the matter of grave and serious theft," the judge began, "I find you—"

But before the sentence could be pronounced, the courtroom was shaken by a sudden clamor. The heavy oak doors swung violently open with all the force of an errant gale and a thunderous crash, an almighty noise assaulting the chamber like a peal of warning from some unseen hand.

All heads turned as an unexpected figure stepped boldly into the room, disheveled yet fiery.

Mr. Hargrove, the jewelry manufacturer and merchant—a man known more for his timid demeanor than for bold proclamations—converged into view, lungs heaving as he struggled to catch his breath.

The eyes of the court flitted toward him, curiosity mingling with disbelief.

"My good sire, Justice, Judge, I sincerely hope I'm not too late, I—I do beseech you—"

Hargrove gasped, his breath catching in a tumultuous exhalation as he peered down at the hat he was clasping tightly in his trembling hands. The hat—oh, that inexplicable object of inquiry and revelation—seemed to be pulsing under the duress of a thousand unspoken truths.

Its owner stood red-faced and bewildered, suspended between apprehension and wonder. "I must speak! I'm afraid I simply cannot allow this grave mistake to unfold without my testimony!"

"Hargrove, hush!" the judge hissed, considerable irritation contorting his lined face. "I'll hear no more testimony. My mind is made up on this matter."

Mr. Blackthorn cast a stern and menacing glare in Hargrove's direction, his eyes smoldering with silent command, as though by the sheer force of his will he might arrest the man's words and bind his tongue in fearful obedience. A sweat was forming on his brow, and his right leg jittered up and down as if it had assumed a life of its own. It was evident he also had much to contribute.

Blackthorn said, "Hargrove, your entrance is thoroughly ill-timed; this court has heard the evidence, and I am quite sure our honorable judge Mr. Justice will not entertain—"

"I beg your pardon!" Hargrove interrupted, raising his hands, hat still clutched in his right hand as though it somehow possessed the power to quell the tumult. "But the fate of this boy rests upon a web of deception woven by powerful men! I cannot remain silent any longer. These are all rotten lies!"

All eyes turned, spellbound, Hargrove only standing straighter.

"You see, I was complicit in a plot—one that your associate Blackthorn orchestrated. I planted the brooch at Blackthorn's behest in hopes of gaining favor. Favor to come at the expense of an innocent. You see, my debt was to be forgiven if I—if I betrayed this blameless boy."

Yelps erupted from the gallery, and even the judge momentarily staggered, his pen falling from his faltering grasp—a metal plume that seemed to oppress history itself.

Hargrove continued, "I watched as the bobbies arrested the youth amid the chaos of that dreadful celebration, and I shall carry this guilt to my grave if I do not speak out! It was I who sought to profit from his downfall! Please, let the boy go free. This is the pure, undeniable truth as I stand here and bear witness before the Lord. Let the accused go."

Scrooge's heart raced, every vein and artery on fire. He simultaneously felt both betrayal and admiration at Hargrove's bold confession.

"Hargrove," the judge muttered, a strange pallor creeping into his cheeks as most of the blood was draining from his head. "You dare implicate Mr. Blackthorn in this skullduggery? A man of such stature and unimpeachable character? You wish to blacken his name?"

"Why, his name is already black, sir, for he is Blackthorn, is he not? It is a matter undeniable!" Hawthorne's pun drew chuckles from the gallery before they stilled again, waiting for the eruption.

Mr. Blackthorn, a practiced air of indignation about him, raised his shoulders ever so slightly, a peacock preening itself. He seemed eager to bask in the much-deserved glow of commendation that he so fancifully believed awaited him. "Clearly, Justice, no one has cause to believe the words of this odd gentleman. I fear he is irretrievably sick. As you rightly say, he has no just cause to question my stature. He is a poor soul, likely to pass away quite soon from an affliction of the brain, Judge. Indeed, just standing here, looking at him, I do think he is suffering delirium or acute corruption of the—"

Hargrove was still contemplating the judge's words and those of that weasel, Blackthorn.

He stared into Blackthorn's face.

"You dare question my aforementioned stature, do you, fine fellow?" he spat out in Blackthorn's direction, his voice rising to a crescendo, everyone spellbound. "Pray, tell me what stature *you* would claim to have? Would it be the stature of a man building his empire upon the backs of the destitute? Would it, Blackthorn? Or would it be the stature of a bully-boy, beating children into submission, not only in the courtroom as we all bear witness, but also in the hidden torture rooms of industry?"

Hargrove gestured emphatically toward Tom, whose countenance dared display a smattering of hope for his reprieve amidst the ongoing tumult. "Mr. Blackthorn has sullied this trial from its inception, and that much you ought to know! I cannot represent the likes of such men any longer!"

The witness, like a worm, had turned before everyone's eyes, and the room fell perfectly still, perfectly silent. If a pin had dropped, everybody would have heard it and jumped.

The judge, now flustered, raised a hand in a weak bid to restore order, but the beauty of truth had already taken flight, soaring upward to strike at the heart of justice itself.

"Forger of falsehoods," Scrooge thundered toward the guilty, then turning to the onlookers. "It is you who bear witness not merely to the guilt or innocence in the child's fate! We have uncovered the very rot plaguing this court! Do you not see? You have the power to unleash justice upon the corrupt!"

With each word, the walls of collusion began to tremble, unveiling a vile spirit long interred.

The hushed crowd filled with murmurs of disbelief, and against the backdrop of Scrooge's rallying cry, sympathy began to swell for the beleaguered Tom.

The judge, a figure of judicial authority swathed in dampening dread, felt the noose of culpability tightening around his own throat, for he bore not only the mantle of his office but also the heavy burden of collusion with the industrialists who had sought to undermine justice's fragile threads.

Nevertheless, he was still determined to deliver a guilty verdict against Tom, viewing it as his only salvation from the impending storm of scrutiny and scandal threatening to unravel the cabal stretching into the dark recesses of his conscience. Yet, as the murmurs of dissent transformed into a crescendo of fury, the crowd seething with indignation at the blatant injustices laid bare before them, an electrifying pulse of insurrection filled the air, sparking vengeful thoughts.

Faced with the prospect of a mob, their intent clearer than the ink on his papers, the judge realized the precariousness of his position. Thus, in a last desperate gambit to salvage his authority, he yielded, allowing Hargrove to take the floor and proceed with his revelations, albeit with the lingering taste of betrayal souring in his throat. He braced for the tempest now hovering on the horizon.

Whether he would be swept away with the criminals he had once called allies or emerge as a champion of justice remained to be seen, but at that moment, the choice felt agonizingly uncertain.

"Proceed, Mr. Hargrove!" the judge blurted, reining in his authority before the swirling tide of public sentiment. "What further accusations do you wish to bring against the industrialists?"

"My accusation stands, and furthermore, I can produce evidence!" Hargrove declared, a fire ignited in him. "There are witnesses who can attest to Mr. Blackthorn's character; I have kept many records, notes of his dealings considerably nearer to the shadows than in the light! The brooch was but one act of a larger scheme to distill fear amongst us, to keep the laborers cowering in submission while he filled his coffers! This is not merely a matter of theft; it is a matter of extortion, and it affects us all!"

The hum of excitement electrified the gallery.

Scrooge sensed that the tide had turned, a boat casting off its moorings while waves crashed against its hull, ushering in a new dawn. The breath of the public depended not merely upon the fate of one boy, but upon the pervasive injustice they had overlooked for too long.

"Your Honor," Scrooge pressed, a master of rhetoric now emboldened. "These revelations should be heard right across London Town! The people deserve to know of the collusion and wretchedness borne of greed! To condemn this innocent boy would be to endorse the villainy seeping into the many hidden crevices of our society! Your Honor, you can save this evil from further spread."

The judge, whose reputation was teetering precariously on the brink of exposure, shuffled uneasily in his seat. "Mr. Hargrove, present your evidence! We will not proceed until the truth is unmasked!"

He turned, casting a furtive glance toward Mr. Blackthorn, who, suffocated by the growing unrest, was seeing the seeds of his power coming under threat. At that moment, he wished the building would come crashing down, hiding him and all his treachery from the eyes presently searing into his soul.

A sweeping wave of hope surged through the room, roaring to life.

Hargrove nodded, determination writ large on his face.

With clenched fists, he marched forward brandishing documents, notes hidden beneath a cloak of obscurity. A murmur of anticipation rippled across the court, already sensing that the moment had arrived for truth to shatter the chains of deceit.

With each passing moment, the vitality of the crowd grew, a chorus clamoring for justice, clashing against the monetary might of the elite.

Scrooge could feel the pulse of change racing through the air, tales of woe once tethering men to despair now twinkling in the eyes of the people, charged with purpose.

"All we seek is fairness!" came a voice from the back, echoing through the hall. "Let our conviction stand against those who will feast upon our labor!"

The judge, foreseeing the dissent brewing even beyond his walls, accepted the documents presented by Hargrove with shaky hands.

"Let us adjourn until these matters can be properly examined and the truth discerned," he finally proclaimed, releasing Tom instantly from the bounds of his confinement.

The boy nearly stumbled forward, reaching out as if to grip with both eager and thankful hands the freedom so promptly gifted back to him. A breath of fresh air was coursing through his young body.

Unchained from the shackles of unjust condemnation, Tom gazed into the faces of his family. They had gathered inside the court, breathless with anxiety, the life once stolen from them returned anew.

And at that moment, a wave of admiration washed over the spectators, cascading their sentiment firmly onto Scrooge's shoulders. Once the icon of misery mightiest, he now stood beaming.

As the courtroom emptied, the tides against the nefarious nature of the industrial elite began swelling higher, cascading through the streets and reshaping public discourse forevermore.

Word commenced spreading like wildfires in dry fields, igniting spirits and sparking calls for change, reaching each corner of society as they sought liberation from the chains of rapacity—much like the very affairs that had constricted Ebenezer Scrooge's heart until but a few short minutes prior.

And so it was that amid the sweeping reforms of a justice awakened, two lives entwined with fate— Tom and Ebenezer Scrooge—emerged from the shadows of despair and stepped into the light, emboldened by their hope and the unyielding desire for righteousness binding them together. United against those who sought to oppress, they would labor to build a brighter future, where innocence would no longer be sacrificed on the altar of greed, but cherished with the reverence it deserved.

Thus, London itself, the grand repository of humanity and ambition, began stitching a new design —a fabric woven not from the thread of corruption but from the golden strands of righteousness, in which all voices might be heard, not one single soul left to languish alone.

Chapter 11: The Final Lesson

As the sun dipped below the horizon, casting an orange glow across the cobblestones, Scrooge and Tom found themselves sauntering side by side, unspoken camaraderie wrapping around them like a cherished woolen blanket. Only a few hours had passed since the weight of injustice had been lifted from Tom's shoulders, leaving behind the vestiges of despair. In a moment of pure exuberance, they embraced, their closeness conveying far more than mere words could ever express.

Scrooge felt the vitality of Tom's spirit, marveling at how the shackles of oppression had given way to the spine of resilience and truth.

"Tom, my boy!" Scrooge declared, releasing him from the embrace but still holding onto his shoulders, a proud paternal glimmer in his eyes. "Your release is not merely a stroke of luck; it is a testament to your strength and an affirmation of your worth! 'Tis a blessing from above, lad, a sign that providence has marked you for a greater purpose, that of restoring equity to this troubled city. See to it, my boy, see that you do not squander this second chance, for such gifts are not bestowed lightly, nor will they ever come again. This has been a battle hard fought, even harder won."

He beamed with admiration, his words ignited by the knowledge of their shared struggle.

Tom smiled, the light of freedom shining bright within him.

"Thank you, Mr. Scrooge. It was your faith and persuasion that guided me through those dark hours. I promise you, I shall never forget it." There was an earnestness in his gaze, one that spoke volumes of the trust and respect they had cultivated amid the chaos of their lives.

As they approached Scrooge's home, the familiar silhouette of his abode stood against the evening sky, the cozy glow of the lamp inside beckoning them. It felt as though the world had shifted on its axis, leaning favorably toward those who dared to dream and inspire.

Scrooge realized, in this newfound exhilaration, how far they had both journeyed from their individual pasts, the burdens they had borne slowly unraveling, freeing their spirits.

"Tom, consider what lies ahead for you," Scrooge mused, stepping onto the stoop, his heart swelling with a sense of possibility as he placed a hand gently on Tom's shoulder. "You hold within you the spark of greatness. With your tenacity and passion for justice, you will one day revolutionize London! This city needs voices like yours—gentle yet firm, determined but understanding."

Tom's eyes widened at the audacity of such a vision.

"You truly believe that, Mr. Scrooge? You honestly believe in me?"

"Indeed, I do," Scrooge replied, his voice steadier than the most resilient brick-and-mortar foundation. "How could I not, having seen the young man you have become? Believe it and strive for it! Influencing the hearts of men and women may seem a heavy task, but you, my dear Tom, are destined to ripple across these streets like the most righteous tide. You are capable."

After they exchanged a knowing look infused with the deepest friendship and mutual respect, Scrooge watched Tom turn to leave, bounding off with the buoyant energy of hope underpinning each step. A pang of nostalgia welled up within Scrooge; in Tom, he saw echoes of his beloved nephew, Fred, whose vibrant spirit still persistently tugged at his thoughts, urging him outward and on.

With a proud smile forming, Scrooge murmured to himself, "Yes, Tom will change this city. He will be the very inspiration that others so desperately seek to guide them! I believe in you, Tom."

The notion bubbled within him, and from this moment on, all former gloom dissipated, making way for the dawn of something fresh and enriched. Now, he could envision a future painted with infinitely brighter hues of justice, beauty and kindness, a veritable masterpiece before the world.

The painting would relate not only their individual stories, but also those of the lives of many who would find their way through the darkness just as Tom had done.

The promise of this new horizon hung big and bold, and with that vision, Scrooge stepped inside his cherished home, the warmth of the gathering evening instantly encompassing him.

It served as a reminder that the world was indeed a grand stage upon which promise and humanity could extend their arms to embrace the naissance of a far more enticing tomorrow.

And it was then, the fervor of the day's events still so fresh, that a sudden gust swept through his foyer, a whisper of something ethereal brushing against Scrooge's cheek like an old forgotten tune.

In shock, he turned as if caught in some spellbinding waltz.

From beyond the threshold of this mundane world, the ghost of Jacob Marley broke forth, freed from his grasping chains and burdens that had once tethered him to a fate wrought of his own misdeeds.

No longer bound by the heavy weights of earthly regret, Marley glowed with an otherworldly light.

"Scrooge!" he hollered, his voice a harmonious blend of encouragement and remorse, sounding clear over through the din of the crowd. "Look at what you have done! Behold the unity forged by love and long-suffering purpose! What a marvel you have created this week!"

Awe-struck, Scrooge's heart filled with a profound sense of purpose as the specter of his erstwhile partner surged closer, his face bright with compassion rather than with the mournful wretchedness once characterizing his appearance. Marley, now appearing as an amiable harbinger of goodwill, extended both hands, waving toward the multitude gathered in a throng under a cloudless sky.

Scrooge felt the connections between them thrumming with life.

"I come not to haunt you but to inform you of the gladdest tidings!" Marley proclaimed in a rush as if all too eager to spit out the words, lest Scrooge could glean the wrong impression from his unexpected visit. His spirit was unmistakably alight with the luminescence of redemption.

"Where once I could only usher in darkness, I am now free to share the fascinating truth of transformation; my eternal work is to help those once ensnared by greed break their chains and rise anew, just as you have! I labor now from beyond the veil, striving to aid all those remaining shackled by the chains of iniquity and the folly of a life squandered in greed and riotous excess.

"My work is to guide them to freedom, that they may forsake the shadows of their past and receive with grace the light of redemption, embracing the child in whose name we celebrate Christmas."

In those fervent declarations, Scrooge understood he was not merely a solitary buoy in tumultuous waters; rather, he was a vital thread in an expansive drive for moral progress, each brave soul intertwined in a shared destiny. With each heartbeat and word that Marley spoke, the marvel of his own rebirth resonated within the hearts of the people, burning away the ashes of despair.

Scrooge beheld Marley's rejoicing spirit. Holding aloft that ethereal figure radiant and glorious amidst the gathering crowd, Scrooge found within himself a swelling, clamorous tide of positivity. He felt as giddy as a schoolboy on holiday, a sensation strikingly akin to that very Christmas morn, long since departed, when the Spirits had wrought their wondrous reclamation upon his soul.

Yet, before he could give voice to the tumultuous thoughts jittering like will-o'-the-wisps within his mind, there came a sudden, insistent knock at the door, shattering the moment's reverie.

In the blink of an eye—swift as a fleeting whisper—Marley's presence vanished, leaving behind naught but the tremors of his newest and most encouraging revelation.

Scrooge stirred toward the door, light as a feather, opening to the knock that summoned him.

The surprising sight he beheld as he opened up was that of a soul in strife, an embodiment of inner turmoil not anticipated. The mayor, once revered and feared in equal measure, now stood before Scrooge with his brow furrowed. The façade of authority so ardently upheld now seemed utterly flimsy, made transparent to the heart of the people he had neglected for far too long.

"Mr. Scrooge!" the mayor uttered, his voice tinged with a tremor betraying deep unease. "I—I seek your counsel. I have come to realize the gravity of my complacency, my entanglement with the industry that has wrought such suffering upon our beloved city and its people."

There was an earnestness in his eyes, a flicker of vulnerability to shatter the rigid mask he had been wearing like armor. The townspeople's cries, cascading like an ethereal melody, had pierced the depths of his conscience, urging forth the reluctant revelations that had lain dormant within him.

"I confess to feeling embarrassed, Mr. Scrooge. Embarrassed by all that I have done. I entered politics with grand aspirations to improve London Town for all its people. Yet, I allowed coin and control to corrupt until I became part of the evil destroying society."

"And you say you … seek my counsel?" Scrooge replied, the weight of the moment more than palpable, emulating the tension in the crowd now gathering outside Scrooge's home. "What counsel do you wish? The counsel that reminds you of the very people you have forsaken, the lives you have traded for dominion and gain? Would it be that kind of counsel you seek? For if not, if I happen to misconstrue, please advise me. Speak plainly, Mayor, for the time for empty niceties is long past."

The mayor appeared discomfited, hopping momentarily foot to foot.

"I—as I said, I feel ashamed … that I know I have stumbled down a path blinded by ambition and the pursuit of substance," the mayor confessed, his face flushed with shame that only the most introspective could bear. "The allure of industry led me astray, a siren song drowning out the more tender plea of humanity's finer qualities. I was so consumed with promises of profit, blinded by dreams of gleaming gains, that I remained deaf and blind to the suffering increasingly spiraling around me. I have you to thank for my clarity of vision now. If not for you, I fear I would have remained quite lost."

Scrooge's heart softened, tempered by the metamorphosis of the man standing in front of him.

Did not every man deserve a second chance?

Perhaps even innumerable chances if he saw and admitted to the error of his ways.

The truth had been laid bare before him.

"Your revelation, though late, is crucial and most welcome," he said with grace, exhibiting the humble man he always had been. "Many have suffered in silence, their burdens carried alone while you were basking in the glow of your authority. But every man, regardless of the chains he once wore, has the power to change course. It takes only the slightest inclination, the most unobtrusive switch.

"It requires nothing other than a promise to oneself, and the will to see it through."

The mayor took a breath, his shoulders constricting as he inhaled the gravity of the moment.

"But if I were to seek your counsel as I said, what would you have me do?" he asked almost pleadingly, taking on the air of a child desperately requiring his father's direction.

"To begin," Scrooge urged, as though each syllable were carved from stone. "Commit to rooting out the corruption blatantly festering within your own office, the backdoor deals that line your pockets and leave the common man bereft. Stand with us against those who cling to power while the masses are left wanting; seek to mend what has long lain broken, speak up for the voiceless, and embrace the future of camaraderie over mammonism."

At this, a flicker of determination ignited in the mayor's eyes, as much a spark of redemption as it was of promise. "Why, how right you are, Ebenezer Scrooge," he replied, his tone forthright now, lips curving into a slight but genuine smile. "I will learn, I will act! I shall not allow the cries of the people to drown in vapid desires. Together, we shall work to undo the wrongs inflicted upon this city!"

In the weeks and months following that fateful night, the air of London began to shift as if touched by a benevolent hand. The mayor, emboldened by Scrooge's unexpected endorsement, became a man transformed, a public servant whose heart had been rudely awakened from its slumber.

Now, it was as though he had changed from a man who was deaf, to one capable of hearing even the smallest, plaintive cry for help from the clamoring voices of the people he had once neglected, the same ones he formerly had deemed too small, too insignificant, too unworthy to fret about.

With indefatigable zeal, he embarked upon a campaign of reform to run alongside his solemn promise to the citizens of London, holding meetings in the city square, where he stood before multitudes with a sincerity dispelling all doubt. "No longer shall we be held captive by the machinations of corrupt men!" he cried out, unafraid, undeterred by the fear of who may hear him.

With every word, he sought to instill faith, to rebuild the tattered bonds withering beneath the weight of greed, rooting out the corrupt coin ruling his city, forming a lattice of trust; though it would be delicate, it would be strong enough to withstand the tempests of change.

In that bustling heart of the city, where once the demons of fear had loomed ubiquitous, the mayor vowed to expose the insidious plots woven by Mr. Blackthorn, that notorious architect of deceit.

This man's talons had been gripping the city's livelihood for far too long.

From dawn till dusk, the mayor labored diligently, enlisting the help of Simon, the earnest clerk whose loyalty to righteousness had not faltered, even in the very darkest of hours.

Together, they navigated the murky swamps of subterfuge characterizing the former regime, gathering testimony, documenting misdeeds, and revealing the murk in which shadows had thrived.

The fateful day of reckoning arrived, a day not merely holding promise.

It was also brimming with the intoxicating possibility of justice.

***

The trial of Mr. Blackthorn opened with a fanfare of anticipation, the entire city alive with an electricity of collective hope. Scrooge, who stood shoulder to shoulder with the mayor, felt the weight of the moment mingling with the lightness of spirit that accompanied belief in redemption.

"My loyal brethren," the mayor proclaimed as he addressed the assembly, "we shall not be cowed by the shadow of tyranny lurking in the blackness! Today, we bind the ties of our unity, for they who have preyed upon us shall face the very same laws they have sought to manipulate!"

The trial itself unfolded like a grand drama, the court a vivid tableau in which the flag of corruption became deftly unraveled thread by thread. Witness after witness emerged from the shadows of silence, and with quaking voices, they recounted their tales of woe—the evictions, the extortion, the scandals, all vices that had flourished unchecked. Each testimony served as a nail in the coffin of Blackthorn's nefarious empire, a legacy built upon suffering and greed that would have no sanctuary in the face of the coming righteousness. Power was rightfully returning to where it belonged, the people!

Mr. Blackthorn, his countenance transformed from bluster to bewilderment, was pronounced guilty of corruption and malfeasance, a fitting end for one peddling in the agonies of the innocent.

The shattering of his cabal was swift and resolute, as those who had once been his accomplices found themselves unceremoniously cast aside, their nefarious dealings laid bare for all to see by the discerning eye of the newly reborn administration.

As Blackthorn was led away in shackles, the air swelled with a triumph surging through the soil of the city, a resplendent affirmation that the chains of tyranny could indeed be broken.

A wave of gratitude enveloped the mayor, who found himself embraced by the citizens he once had neglected, their faces buoyed with rekindled trust and unwavering admiration.

"You have shown us the way, Mayor!" they proclaimed, their cheers rising, sounding through the streets like the sound of a newfound spring. "You have supported us, Mayor! We salute you!"

In the weeks that unfurled into months, the fruits of labor continued blossoming in the hallowed alleys and bustling market squares, where voices once stifled now rang with laughter and purpose.

The mayor's tireless endeavors bore witness to the resurrection of community spirit, and under Scrooge's watchful eye—now not merely a man changed but also a deeply compassionate soul—both leaders forged a partnership grounded in hope and community.

Thus, the contours of London shifted toward the light, unfurling like petals of a long-dormant bloom as the people of this steadfast city enthusiastically grasped their destiny's reins.

Oppression's shadows were receding as the fruits of their shared toil began to flourish into a vast show of humanity. It held aloft the ideals of justice, benevolence, and kinship, vital elements at the core of a society reborn. They nurtured the unwavering knowledge that together, they had defeated darkness, emerging into a dawn rich with possibilities as yet undreamed.

***

On a glorious Christmas Day, the city was vibrant with life; witness to the joyous spirit lovingly nurtured over the year gone by. The air was thick with the laughter of children playing in the streets, the scent of roasting geese wafting from cheerful households, the soft songs of carolers ringing out.

Yet, within the gentle confines of a modest yet warm bedchamber, a different sort of stillness prevailed; a profound reverence settled over the room, peace and reflection befitting the occasion.

In that chamber lay Ebenezer Scrooge, now a venerable old man, his once sharp features softened by the passage of time, each line and wrinkle a chronicle of a life rich in transformation.

The flickering candles danced with a grace befitting of nature itself, their flames bending tenderly toward him as if they too were mindful of the magnitude of the moment unfolding. Scrooge lay beneath a pile of blankets, his eyes closed yet brimming with serene contemplation, a tranquil expression adorning his face. Was he dreaming of memories so beautifully coloring his later years?

Gathered around him, for it was indeed a day of love and solemnity, were those who had come to embody devotion and kinship. Lily, Fred's widow, her heart swaddled in the bittersweet threads of loss and relatively newfound peace, sat at his side with her children— bright-eyed, giggling youths—nurtured in a world also heartily transformed through Scrooge's resolution.

They whispered gentle stories of merriment, weaving in memories of Fred and the radiant love that had nourished their family, their chatter mingling with the soft creak of the floorboards; it was as though even the most minuscule sounds in the room held onto an air of sacred reverence, breathing it out anew to fill the atmosphere and Scrooge's lungs with positivity and good health.

Across the way, Bob Cratchit and his beloved son, Tim, whose spirit had soared after adversity's vanquishment, were standing vigilant. Tim, now a vital and sturdy figure, moved closer to the bedside, coming to rest a warm hand on Scrooge's chest.

"Mr. Scrooge, my second father," he murmured, his voice infused with a tenderness that stirred the ether in the room, his eyes moist. "You are the reason we are whole. You are the heart of us."

Scrooge had not merely been a benefactor; he had transformed their lives a thousandfold.

And lo! The room seemed to hold its breath, resonating with an unearthly stillness as the esteemed mayor, that beacon of renewed civic duty, also duly entered the sanctuary of Scrooge's chamber.

A figure of dignity and integrity these days, he offered a gentle bow.

He too, like all present, recognized the profound impact this man had had, not merely on their own lives, but upon London itself.

He clasped Scrooge's frail hand, offering a gesture of solidarity between one who had once lost his way and another who had latterly reclaimed his light.

As Scrooge lay enveloped in a shifting twilight's tender embrace, a soft sound began to swell from the streets beyond his window, a harmonious blend of voices rising in unity as the citizens of London gathered outside his home, showing boundless love and gratitude, paying last respects.

With sincere and heartfelt reverence, they raised their voices in the timeless carol, "What Child is This?" each note a warm caress to the dying man's spirit.

A poignant refrain reached his ears, though he never stirred.

> *"Nails, spear shall pierce him through,*
> *The Cross be borne for me, for you;*
> *Hail, hail the Word Made Flesh,*
> *The babe, the son of Mary!"*

Then there was dear Tom, his youthful countenance marred by teardrops blurring his vision, cascading like gentle droplets of rain on a far too thirsty, parched, forgotten earth.

An ache of profound sorrow lodged itself within him.

He fully grasped that his beloved mentor was poised to embark upon the next step in this grand, inexorable scheme of life, the greatest odyssey known to man, that of mystery and transcendence.

Words faltered on his lips, caught in the delicate web of emotion threatening to ensnare him.

Leaning over the aged figure of Scrooge, who lay there imbued with the quiet dignity of a life well-lived, he tenderly caressed the rough-hewn cheek and pressed a soft, loving kiss to his forehead.

No greater affection and reverence could a young heart muster.

With each ounce of courage summoned from the depths of his soul, he half-whispered, his voice barely rising above the tender hush of the room, "I love you, dear Ebenezer Scrooge. Like you, I shall honor Christmas in my heart and strive to keep its spirit alive throughout all the seasons of the year.

"I will live as you have shown me, in the Past, the Present, and the Future."

How sweetly those words kissed the air, tender as a crystalline snowflake.

In those final moments, the weight of time bearing down upon him, Scrooge breathed deeply, filling his lungs with the fragrance of the festive season that wafted in through the narrowly opened window, ajar like a weary eye—the laughter, the love, life itself blooming anew.

A tranquil smile somehow succeeded in gracing his exhausted lips as he opened his eyes to find those he cherished most gathered in a circle around the bed.

His heart set off fluttering with the knowledge that indeed, he had left a great legacy, a world colored not with the shades of misanthropy but with the vibrant hues of humanity.

With an exhalation seeming to carry throughout the ages, a soft release transporting with it all the weariness of the age just passed, Scrooge slipped gently and easily from that mortal realm.

In that sacred moment, the room bowing in hushed reverence, flickering candles shimmering brighter as though acknowledging the significance of his demise, even the air whispered its humble breath of gratitude. Memories of the man once dwelling among them as little more than a shadow now grew luminous, another small but infinite star joining the great and vast celestial display.

And as his final breath wove its way into the annals of history, the gathering felt a sudden, inexplicable shift; there came forth a warmth and a light that appeared to transcend the bounds of mortality, a promise that his spirit would live on, eternally woven into the hearts of those he had touched. The happening stirred within each of them an enduring call to kindness and generosity of spirit, to become the man the great maker had intended, staying true to righteousness' path.

His mortal existence dissipating into hushed whispers, Ebenezer Scrooge slowly transcended beyond life itself, meeting a splendid tableau in which the spirits of his dearly departed gathered with an affection transcending the boundaries of earthly concept of time.

The Wanderer, forever a figure of ethereal grace, stood at the forefront exuding warmth and acceptance, while Jacob Marley, now unshackled from the burdens of too many earthly regrets, radiated his astonishingly joyous redemptive light.

Scrooge's mother, her features pinked with love, joined hands with sweet Fan, whose laughter made the sound of chimes in the cool evening air. Fred, ever the beacon of mirth, and Scrooge's father, softened by years' passage and truth's clarifying light, stood proudly beside them, all looking youthful, in the very best of health.

Together, they formed a circle of familial bliss, radiant smiles weaving unity's own image.

Whatever that elusive Christmas Spirit truly was, no one could have denied it still cast its light over a multitude of souls, forever binding them in celestial embrace. Here, they opened their arms, welcoming him home to a realm where love conquered all sorrow and kinship reigned eternal.

Though time had claimed Ebenezer Scrooge in the self-same way as it would come to claim all mortals, his passing was not met with mourning.

The day of his funeral was a time of remembrance, not sorrow, a time of uplift and rejoicing, a celebration of a life lived for others and of a man turned to love.

People from all walks of life gathered to honor the man who once had been hardened by greed and fear but who had transcended all sins and afflictions.

Songs filled the air, the bells of all London's churches ringing in joyful peals.

Thus, the name of Ebenezer Scrooge became inscribed into the city's soul, a testament to the boundless power of regeneration—the inexorable truth that, in the end, only love may redeem and uphold, ever guiding vulnerable humankind safely through time's fleeting shadows.

Epilogue

Many years had passed since Ebenezer Scrooge had walked London's streets as a solitary figure shunning his fellow men. Just as Yuletide's heart had redeemed him, so too did the city regenerate itself; though still necessarily clothed in the garments of industry, these days, it proudly bore a far kinder countenance. Tall chimneys were still puffing plumes into the sky, but among the soot and toil, there existed harmony, giving and mutual care, exhaling merciful beneficence into the metropolis.

Scrooge's charitable foundations, borne of his later years and nurtured by the hands of the thousands he had mentored, had grown into towering examples of altruism and promise for the future.

Schools for the poor were flourishing now, their halls filled with the sounds of merrymaking and learning. Orphanages once steeped in despair were now places of comfort, and even the formerly cruel workhouses had become sanctuaries offering reform.

Fred's children, now grown, willingly acted as staunch stewards of his legacy.

They spoke of their great-uncle not only as a man who had changed his own life but also as one who had bettered countless others. The tale of Scrooge's redemption and his unwavering mission became a parable, told by firelight on Christmas Eve to children with shiny eyes and eager hearts.

Amidst this thriving tableau of compassion and renewal had risen the indomitable figure of Tom, once a humble boy cradled in the warmth of Scrooge's redemption, now a man of kind vision.

With an energy ignited by his mentor's teachings, Tom had ascended to the illustrious office of Mayor of London, a mantle to wear with both humility and purpose.

His leadership, marked by a steadfast commitment to the welfare of all, was causing fresh ripples of transformation to spread throughout the city.

Under his stewardship, the streets were growing brighter with festivity, and the hearts of the citizens were swelling with a shared sense of responsibility and pride. Housing projects were burgeoning, providing safe havens for families, and initiatives to educate the city's youth were flourishing too, ensuring that every child received the chance to thrive. Tom's unwavering dedication to the ideals instilled in him by Scrooge had become the bedrock of a new London.

Tom had emerged not merely as a leader, but equally, as a living testament to the possibilities within a heart willing to embrace the timeless spirit of Christmas and the child for whom it was celebrated, forever altering the trajectory of a city that would flourish in joy and unity for generations to come.

Yet, amidst his many triumphs, Tom carried the memory of Scrooge close to his heart, visiting the grave of his benefactor with a reverent frequency. In a quiet corner of the cemetery, beneath the shade of a stately oak, a simple headstone marked his resting place.

The inscription read:

Ebenezer Scrooge: A man who, in embracing the spirit of Christmas, found redemption, inspired hope, and kindled a flame of compassion that burns eternal.

In the stillness of the cemetery, he would share his successes and dreams, his voice barely above a whisper in recounting victories and challenges alike.

With each visit, he felt Scrooge's influence, a presence beckoning him onward, reminding him that nothing good ever came in the absence of the will to invest both dedication and boundless hard work.

Beneath the shade of that stately oak, Tom would pause before the simple headstone, thankful for the generosity that had forever altered his path and the lives of countless others.

Even in death, Scrooge continued to give.

His Last Will and Testament left no room for hoarding wealth but instead directed nearly all his fortunes to the betterment of the city once disdained. He, in his magnanimity, bequeathed ample means to dearest Lily and her tender progeny, ensuring that they might flourish and thrive, shielded from the harsh vicissitudes of life's fickle fortune. Scrooge's charitable works also continued, carried forward by a new generation inspired by his deeds and meritorious teachings.

There were still trials and tribulations, for human frailty could never wholly be eradicated, but there was also a prevailing sense of unity and a shared understanding that Christmas was not confined to a single day. It was an illumination to guide all days, showing in no uncertain terms what humanity could be when it chose love over greed, kindness over apathy, fruitfulness over bleakness.

Thus, the story of Ebenezer Scrooge came to its rightful end, not with the extinguishing of a life, but with a beautiful enduring legacy. For as long as Christmas' spirit perpetuated in the hearts of the people, Scrooge's work would continue on.

In that truth lay the greatest succor of all, the imaginings of a familiar, beloved hushed voice proclaiming, "God bless us, every one."